ISLAND FEVER

By

ESMERELDA SNODGRASS

Hutton Electronic Publishing
Westport

ISBN   978-09888775-5-9

The cover art is taken from a play produced under the auspices of the WPA in Harlem, NY in 1938, entitled Haiti by William DuBois and is in the collection of the author.
Cover & interior design by Katie Johnson

Published by
Huttonelectronicpublishing.com
160 North Compo Road, Westport, CT 06880-2102
Manufactured in the United States of America

To Toussaint L'Ouverture

TOUSSAINT, the most unhappy man of men!
Whether the whistling Rustic tend his plough
Within they hearing, or thy head be now
Pillowed in some deep dungeon's earless den; -
O miserable Chieftain! Where and when
Wilt thou find patience? Yet die not; do thou
Wear rather in thy bonds a cheerful brow:
Though fallen thyself, never to rise again,
Live and take comfort. Thou hast left behind
Powers that will work for thee; air, earth, and skies;
There's not a breathing of the common wind
That will forget thee; thou hast great allies;
Thy friends are exultations, agonies,
And love and man's unconquerable mind.

William Wordsworth

ISLAND FEVER

Table of Contents

Chapter One

The Voyage

An Atlantic gale tore through the rigging, sending all the sheets into an eerie chorus resembling nothing more than a high, wailing whine. What sails were still in place flapped heavily in the wind, sending *L'Ocean* plunging and wallowing in the deep troughs thrown up by the vast ocean and the wild storm through which the enormous fleet, sent by Napoleon ploughed toward Hispaniola and the slave uprising of San-Domingue.

Spaced out alongside and flowing behind the flagship of the great flotilla were the other ships of Napoleon's fleet, which had put out from Brest, Rochefort, Toulon, Cadiz and Lorient in France, and Vlissinden in Holland, heading southwest across the wintery Atlantic. Where 20,000 soldiers, with an equal number of sailors, were to put down the takeover of the island by former slaves, led by their colorful and charismatic leader, Toussaint L'Ouverture. A brilliant and intelligent warrior, he had won the loyalty of the local chiefs and trained a large army of guerrilla soldiers as well. The National Convention of 1794 at the beginning of the French Revolution had granted freedom to all slaves of San Domingue, as well as all the other French colonies in the Caribbean.

It was Napoleon's purpose, in sending his fleet, to put down the uprising of the former slaves, take over the French portion of the island, and reinstate slavery. The goal was to take over the incredible sugar production of this island, and win the revenues from it back for France.

Sumptuous quarters had been prepared for the French leader of this expedition, his wife and young son, but on this terrible winter afternoon, the hatches were battened down against the storm and the inhabitants of the main cabin were dreadfully, disgustingly, seasick.

Pauline Bonaparte Leclerc, favorite sister of Napoleon and wife of the expeditionary forces leader, General Leclerc, lay moaning in her bunk. Her lady in waiting, Odette Boucher, wiped Pauline's sweaty brow with a linen napkin, dipped in the tepid water that was all that was available at the time. As Pauline retched for the umpteenth time that afternoon, Odette held up a basin to her lips to catch any vomit. Only a thin stream of bile emerged from Pauline's lips; she had emptied her stomach of any food she might have consumed some hours ago.

The lady in waiting was as lushly dark as Pauline was fair. Indeed, the two women could not have presented more of a contrast. Napoleon's sister was a dainty doll of a woman, tiny and perfectly proportioned, with beautiful hands and feet, and milk white skin, which she kept in its alabaster perfection with daily baths of milk, when she could get it. Obviously, on shipboard, such luxury was unavailable to her and she had to make do with daily sluices of sea water, warmed for her ablutions in the cramped kitchens of the ship, much to the cook's inconvenience. However, inconvenience to others was something Pauline had not considered, at least not since her brother's rapid rise from General, to a member of the Directory, now First Consul of France. Her caprices were beginning to be felt, but no one dared gainsay her every wish; such was the reverence and fear of her brother.

Another feature of shipboard life which, to Pauline was even more vexatious than the sea-water baths, was the lack of privacy to pursue hot, frequent sex with her husband, General Leclerc. It had been necessary sometimes to find a quiet corner of the deck where her husband could throw her skirts up over her arms, and take her standing up, quickly and – for the most part – unsatisfactorily. They had managed a few longer trysts in the main cabin, which they shared, though their own staff as well as the many men needed to sail the vessel were always close by. But, when necessary, they would bolt their door, tear off their clothes and fling caution to the winds. Their noisy lovemaking could be heard around the ship, and many a sailor would pause in his duties and give the universal symbol of fucking: the middle finger inserted within the joining of the thumb and index finger and plunged up and down, with a wink to a fellow swabbie. Alone in their quarters, the Leclercs paid no attention.

One night, early in the voyage, Pauline and Leclerc managed to be alone. She bolted the door and undulated across the swaying deck toward her husband, dropping her diaphanous peignoir behind her, standing at their bunk, slung from the ceiling to accommodate the movement of the ship. She held out one slim, perfect hand, drawing her husband to her.

Dressed in a loose robe over his under-drawers, almost ready for bed, Leclerc needed no urging. He swept up the body of his naked wife and tossed her into their bunk. Giggling, she reached for him, wrapping his strong male body in a tight embrace, pulling his head down to her perfect breasts. Those breasts would later be immortalized by Canova in a marble statue, commissioned by her second husband, the Prince Borghese. Now, at age twenty, they were perfection, firm and round, two perfect mounds of white flesh, topped by small, rosy nipples. Leclerc took one in his mouth, tonguing and sucking, first at one nipple, then the other. He took her hand and placed it on his rampant penis, urging her on. Pauline needed no such encouragement; her tiny fingers stroked and caressed the swinging meat, bringing it to full erection. The pair needed little more in the way of foreplay, and Leclerc mounted his wife, sliding the length of his hard-on into the slippery interior of her vagina, pumping away with gusto until she thrashed beneath him in the beginnings of her first orgasm. With mounting tension he sped up his rhythm, pounding deeper and ever deeper into Pauline's welcoming cunt. Just as he heard her moan in pleasure, he shot forth his sperm into her, letting out a shout of triumph as he did so. He slipped out, sperm mingling with her cum, and heard her sigh softly.

This was but a preliminary bout, one which would resume shortly, as soon as he could achieve another erection, which was not long in coming. Pauline was an expert at foreplay, never letting her sexual partner have much down time between one act of intercourse and the next, as Leclerc knew well.

He lay back in the bunk, prepared to be pleasured by his wife. Pauline complied instantly, stretching her small, slight body on top of his, writhing and wiggling against his chest, his thighs, until his limp penis began to show signs of life again. Smiling, she reached down for the now flaccid organ, stroking and pulling it, running her fingers around the ridge, cupping his balls systematically, tickling the ever so sensitive strip of skin between them and his anus, poking an experimental finger in that opening. She knew her power over men, her expertise in titillating and tormenting them until they rammed home into her slippery pussy, bringing them both to the gates of paradise and beyond. Leclerc squirmed under her, and she flipped around, positioning herself over him, lowering herself ever so slowly until she was able to take his prick in her mouth, and present the sweet lips of her labia to him in return. Together they commenced sucking and licking, until Pauline thought she would climax then and there, no need for full penetration with what had become, thanks to her ministrations, a most satisfactory hard on. She brought herself up to a sitting position and, back to his face, lowered herself onto the length and breadth of her husband's penis, rocking back and forth and squeezing her well developed pelvic muscles as she did so. She heard Leclerc groan, a sound somewhere between pain and pleasure, and redoubled her efforts, fingering her clitoris with a practiced finger as she did so. His groans became louder, and, as her own rapture intensified, animal sounds emanated from her throat, becoming primal screams of pleasure as she rose up, up and ever upward toward the heavens, her orgasm crashing and erupting inside of her. In counterpart, she heard her husband give a shout of triumph underneath her, as together they found mutual orgasm, then release. For a few moments they lay panting side by side, until Pauline again started her ministrations that would prepare for him to enter her for the third time in a half hour. Down the hatchways and on the deck above, sailors paused to listen and to leer. But for the two down in the main cabin, nothing mattered but the sensations they were able to cull one from the other, as they sought the heights of passion, over and over again.

Branded a nymphomaniac later in life, Pauline needed sex as most people need air: all the time. Indeed, she often wore out her young husband with her insatiable sexual demands. And when he was away fighting for Napoleon – which was often – she was perfectly happy to take a series of lovers to slake her quite insatiable need for sex.

These intense bouts of lovemaking did not last long into the voyage, however, for the Atlantic became rough and choppy as gales swept down from the north, and any thoughts of sex flew away with the gale, as the ship ploughed its way toward the Azores, which would be their last port of call before entering the Southern Atlantic and sailing toward Hispaniola. Leclerc and Pauline would become so seasick that nothing else could enter their respective consciousness, as she retched and tossed in the bunk, now a sickbed, not a love couch. Oddly enough their young son, Dermide, as well as the Lady in waiting, Odette were not affected by the roll and toss of the ship and remained perfectly well throughout the voyage.

The lady holding the basin had been born on the island to which they were traveling was a lovely Creole, with almost jet black hair, dark eyes and nearly olive skin. She was taller than Pauline and fuller in figure, a luscious, voluptuous golden goddess. It was partly to serve Pauline, partly to check up on her family's former plantation that she had agreed to make this arduous trip of six weeks duration. It would keep them on the island of Hispaniola for at least several years, taking all members of the expedition away from Paris, the height of civilization. They would disembark on a tropical island, set down in the blue hills and overgrown jungles of Hispanola, among the chattering monkeys, poisonous snakes and guerrilla troops of L'Ouverture. But Odette had not been home since leaving as a young child, taken to Paris to be brought up by an aunt of her fathers, and educated as an upper class

French girl should be. So this chance to return, even in the middle of a revolution seemed heaven sent, and she had agreed to go as Pauline's Lady in waiting without further thought.

Her own husband, Rene Boucher, was an aide de camp to General Leclerc, though this fact had not figured in her decision to attend the General's lady. She and Boucher had entered into an arranged marriage, not one that had worked out very well. At least, on shipboard, she rarely saw him, as he was quartered with the other officers below decks while she occupied a tiny chamber, a cubby hole really, off the main cabin shared by the Leclercs. There was truly no place on the ship for the Bouchers to have sex, which was fine with Odette. The last such encounter with her husband had been the night before they sailed, in the upper chamber of a crude room in a waterfront inn in Brest. There they had slept the night before embarking on this great adventure, there her husband had claimed his conjugal rights as a husband, knowing there would be no further opportunity until they arrived in San Domingue.

It was stuffy in the little chamber, though with a winter storm battering the one small window it was not prudent to open the sash. Night air was known for its noxious properties so the air remained stale and smelled of recent occupants. Odette eyed the lumpy bed with distaste. She would have liked to lie down in her traveling cloak, on top of the grimy bedclothes, and spend her last night on land alone with her thoughts. Such was not to be, of course. She knew Rene would want to use her, take her for his own pleasure while she lay beneath him like a corpse. She did not have long to wait.

Rene shut the door behind them and placed the one wavering candle he carried in its grimy holder on a small table by the bed. He threw off his own cloak, letting it fall over the end of the bed, and began to unfasten the stiff collar of his uniform. Beneath was a flowing linen shirt, then his tight white britches then his drawers, then ... nothing. Odette turned away slightly and peered out the dirty window at the swirling snow.

"Hurry, woman," Rene told her. "It's freezing in here. Prepare yourself for your husband."

She knew better than to protest; indeed the one time she had done so, early in their marriage, he had cuffed her and pushed her down onto the bed. Sighing, she began to undo her own laces, removing her traveling dress of warm cashmere, then her stockings and shoes, finally her chemise. She kept her cloak on, only removing it to slide into the bed, shuddering at the thought of those who had occupied it before her. Rene was already in the other side, lying on his side, waiting. She lay on her back, arms crossed on her chest, legs together at the ankles.

He pried her arms apart, laying them at her sides, then pushed her knees apart with a rough hand. With no preliminaries, he mounted her, forcing her legs apart with his knee, then taking his stiff prick in one hand and guiding it into her shrinking vagina. She wanted to scream, to gag, to roll out from under him and run from the room, but, knowing none of this was possible, lay still and let him get on with it. Hopefully, he would be quick tonight, would ram his penis over and over again into her unwilling cunny, shoot forth his sperm, roll off her and start snoring. Tonight he muttered in her ear, just before ejaculating 'May tonight make a fine son. God knows there will be no opportunity again for a long time." He finished with her, withdrew the now limp and sticky penis, rolled over and went to sleep. In the dark and cold, Odette was a long time before she, too, drifted off, on the last night for six long weeks on dry land.

The pier, on the morning of departure, was rife with sailors loading the ships for the expedition, soldiers in their pristine uniforms forming up to embark, officers barking orders right and left and, to further compound the chaos of sailing out on the evening tide, was the immense mountain of baggage belonging to the leader of this force, General Leclerc. Most of this pile, however, belonged to Pauline, who knew she would be unable to buy any more fripperies so dear to hear heard for many months – perhaps many years – to come. She had outfitted herself for this exile from home with mountains and bales of dresses, shawls, negligees, shoes, stockings, chemises, hats and gloves, enough for several years if no replacements were available during that time. Her maid was wringing her hands, exhorting the sailors who were hustling all the luggage up the gangways of *L'Ocean* not do drop anything, for Madame would have her head if anything was lost or otherwise damaged. Where they would store most of it was a mystery, for the officers' quarters of the ship, which had been completely made over for the Leclerc party, had little storage space. The trunks and other baggage would have to go into the farthest depths of the hold, from where they were not likely to emerge until they arrived at their destination. Pauline would be left with very little in the way of a wardrobe, with no way of having any of her things washed out or ironed for most of the voyage. True, they would call briefly at the Azores for fresh water and food, and there would be laundresses on shore who could cleanse the garments of the General's lady. It would be a long month or more before they arrived at their final destination, during which time Pauline would have no clean clothes at all. It would be a voyage to be endured as best as could be, with unwashed bodies and the smell of vomit permeating everything.

Finally, a half hour before sailing, all was stowed away for the voyage, goodbyes were said on the dock, and *L'Ocean* stood ready to sail out with the tide, leading the flotilla toward Hispaniola and adventure.

Odette gazed around at her cramped quarters, a tiny space off the main cabin, only separated from it by a slatted door, through which she could hear everything that went on in the quarters shared by Pauline and Leclerc. On the other side was an equally small space for the Leclercs' two year old son, Dermide, which he had to share with his governess, the two sleeping in small bunk beds, one above the other. For sanitary arrangements there was a chamber pot in each of the three cabins, but so close together were they, that the inhabitants could easily hear the peeing and shitting of all five of them. For washing, pots of water were carried in morning and night, but only filled with sea water. The precious fresh had to be conserved for the many thirsty mouths on shipboard and could only be replenished if there was rain. For this reason unexpected squalls and storms were to be welcomed, though they tossed the vessels about unmercifully, making stomachs all the more prone to seasickness.

The start of the voyage had been more propitious. Good weather prevailed for the first few days after the flotilla sailed out into the north Atlantic and the novelty of being on shipboard had not worn off. The passengers lolled in specially built deck chairs on the after deck, surrounded by the activity and noise prevalent on any sailing ship of the era: the shouts of the officers, the creaking of the masts and sails, the bells that bonged for every passing hour. And, for a day or two out from land, the cry of the sea birds overhead reminded everyone that they would soon head out into the tractless ocean, as the birds became fewer and fewer then disappeared altogether.

Soon, however, the dreaded pitch and roll of the ships began, as gale force winds blew down from the north, and almost all the passengers took to their berths and became totally, dreadfully, seasick. For two weeks they vomited and retched, totally miserable, unable to do anything for themselves. The few able bodied among them had to take care of the sick ones, holding basins, sponging down feverish bodies, cleaning up the sick and the mess as best they could. Indeed, many of those suffering wished devoutly they had never signed on for this expedition, some even called for death to end their suffering.

Almost two long weeks later the fleet drew into the safe harbors of the Azores, where they anchored in order to replenish the water and food supplies for the long reach, which would last a month or more, across the wide Atlantic to their ultimate destination.

In the main cabin, Pauline Leclerc finally lifted her head. Her always slender body was thin to the point of emaciation; Leclerc was not much better. But the ship was at last in tranquil waters and it was time to rise and make an effort to return to the world.

Odette, together with Mme. Leclerc's personal maid, Marie Claire, who had been as sick as her mistress, rummaged through what luggage had been allowed in the cabin for a decent costume for her mistress to wear as she went ashore. Everything was damp and wrinkled, and almost everything was in need of laundering and pressing, two activities that simply were not possible on shipboard. The two women strung up on a line across their part of the after deck, a pair of flesh colored pantaloons, a chemisette and a day dress, made of finest muslin with the fashionable Greek trim along the neck and hem. The garments fluttered and danced in the balmy breezes of the Azores, shaking off most of the wrinkles and drying the dampness that had hung over all these last two weeks on the storm tossed ocean.

Once Pauline was dressed to go ashore, Odette made her own toilette, donning the least rumpled of her own dresses and followed her mistress, on the arm of the general, ashore. Left behind, Marie Claire bundled a huge amount of laundry together for washing and ironing on shore. There would not be another such opportunity until they reached their final destination on Hispaniola. A carriage, sent by the governor general of the islands, was waiting on the quay, which quickly drove the General's party through the lovely town of Punta Delgarda, with its palm lined streets and fine houses, over which grew a profusion of tropical flowers: bougainvillea, ginger, and frangipani. The road led up to the Palace, where the party was received with due ceremony by the governor general and his lady, who hosted a spectacular banquet for the visitors with all the gentry of the island in attendance. It was good to be on dry land, if only for a couple of days, and to get the land legs which had been absent onboard ship. Sadly, it was soon time to continue on their way. This was not a pleasure cruise and the purpose of the voyage was never far from Leclerc's mind.

Pauline's now pristine laundry was returned to the ship an hour before sailing, and the fleet weighed anchor and sailed away eastward toward the Caribbean and the purpose of this expedition: to put down the uprising in Hispaniola.

Once clear of the Azores, and in the south Atlantic, the weather tempered and seasickness was, at most, mild. There were still over

3,000 miles of ocean to sail before reaching their destination. Pauline managed to spend much of each day on deck, enjoying the warmer weather. Soon, however, the tedium of life on shipboard for passengers overcame her, and her always capricious nature came to the fore.

She demanded Odette read to her for hours on end, and take her dictation as well, in endless letters to be sent home when the opportunity arose – to her mother, Mme Lezetia, her brother, Napoleon and her many friends and family members left behind when they abandoned Europe for an indefinite time. She played with her almost three year old son, Dermide, soon tiring of his childish games, when she sent him back to his governess. And, always, she expected Leclerc to dance attendance on her, for sex to while away many the dreary hour and now she was no longer queasy with seasickness, she demanded more and more.

Leclerc, while enjoying the favors of his wife almost as much as she did of him, had much to attend to, however. He had constant meetings with his staff officers, planning their campaign once they arrived at their destination, and wrote letters back to his brother in law in Paris, telling him of their future plans. In retribution, Pauline took to flirting with the officers traveling with her husband, and even eyed some of the seamen with interest as they went about their duties keeping the ship trimmed and on course. Odette, as lady in waiting, kept her own counsel, praying nothing would flare up to distract Leclerc from his mission. She spent as much time as she could on deck, the better to leave some privacy for the couple in their cabin, to which Pauline lured her husband at all odd hours of the day. She wanted him for everything from a quick fuck, peignoir spread out on the bed under her, while Leclerc, britches down pumped madly away into her streaming cunt, anything to satisfy her ever mounting needs, to a honeyed hour or more of serious lovemaking. But whatever her husband managed, it was never enough. More than once Odette had entered her mistress's quarters, after the general had left – more often than not fastening his britches as he went – to find Pauline, spread eagled on the bed, her own fingers working

11

their magic within her spread labia, stroking and caressing the tender clitoris to bring herself to orgasm. Rather than stop in her self ministration, Pauline always brought herself to full satisfaction before turning to address her lady in waiting.

While Odette had hoped that, on shipboard, she would be free of the infrequent demands of Rene, it was not to be. From time to time her husband tracked her down and marched her off to a remote part of the ship, where he pulled down her pantaloons, flipped up her skirts and lifted her weight easily in his arms, then pushed his not very impressive erection into her dry vagina. More than once they had been seen, by a passing officer or sailor, as he rammed himself into her, grunting like a pig with his efforts. Odette was hard pressed to keep her composure when she encountered the officer or sailor who had caught them, lifting her head high and keeping her eyes forward. Her mistress, had no such scruples, and took it when and where she could, the more frequent the couplings the better.

Nights were the worst for Odette. Separated from the main cabin by the thinnest of partitions, she could hear everything that went on between Pauline and Leclerc.

One particularly warm night, she was having trouble falling asleep, when she heard the general enter the cabin where his wife waited, primed and ready for him.

"Ah, my love," cried Pauline as she spied Leclerc in the doorway. "I have waited so long for you. Come to me, fuck me, fill me up."

"Your wish, Madam, is my command," growled Leclerc, crossing the cabin to the swinging bed where Pauline lay, the lightest of shawls draped provocatively over her nakedness.

"Touch me here," she took his hand and placed it on her black bush. "Kiss me here," she pushed a finger into her sopping pussy, "fuck me until I scream."

"All in good time, cherie, all in good time." Leclerc pulled his shirt out of his waistband, preparing to disrobe and join his wife.

She sat up, shawl falling away from her perfect breasts. "Let me help you." With wild abandon she literally tore the shirt from his body, tossing it carelessly to the floor. She bent and unfastened the buckles at the knees of his britches, then unbuttoned the front flap, pulling one of these buttons loose in her haste to get to her husband's genitals. Panting with the effort, she pushed the offending garment over his knees, trapping Leclerc so he was unable to move, though his penis, beneath the loose under britches, was beginning to strain the linen front. Almost angrily she attempted to push the underwear after the britches, thoroughly trapping her husband in folds of linen.

"Slowly, my love," he told her. "I can't do much encumbered by all these clothes. Let me remove them properly."

"I can't wait," she breathed, as her head went down to nuzzle the now firm prick under its layers of material. "I want you now. I need you now." Her hand groped under the underwear feeling for the hot piece of meat beneath, longing to bring it forth so her husband could ram it home into her twitching, boiling-hot snatch.

Laughing, Leclerc stood up for a moment, pushing the offending garments to the floor. He removed his shoes, the pushed all over his ankles, kicking everything to the floor. Naked, except for his long, ribbed stockings, he rejoined Pauline on the bed, ready for a night of unbridled passion.

Her need for him was so great that she immediately mounted him, thrusting her open labia toward the protruding schlong that bobbed so tantalizingly beneath her. With practiced fingers, she took the engorged organ and guided it into her, twisting and writhing in the beginnings of a mutually satisfying orgasm, as she bore down on her husband, clutching him with the well developed muscles of her vagina.

So well in tune were these two that it took but a few moments for the first of several orgasms to wrack their bodies with ripples of pleasure that turned into loud moans and groans of animal proportions as each bore the other up to that place of mutual release and delight, soaring higher and ever higher into the stratosphere, until both reached the zenith then slowly came back down to earth. They lay sides by side, panting after the exertions, for only a few moments. Pauline began her ministrations of her husband again.

She ran her beautiful, tiny hand down his well muscled chest, parting the hair gently with her fingers, pinching each nipple in its turn until they stood at attention, before continuing downward and ever downward. The white fingers stroked and kneaded ever so gently the bulge of his stomach, then continued downward, encountering the springy patch of his blonde bush, from which the beginnings of another erection was stirring.

"Ah, my little man," she cooed, enclosing his penis in her hand and starting to squeeze and stroke it rhythmically. "My beautiful, precious little man. Mine, all mine." She stepped up her efforts, wringing a low moan from her husband.

"Now me for you," he managed to breathe. "Let me feel your beautiful tits, your hairy protuberance, the lips you keep just for me." His own hand began to play over her body, following the same path she had just traced on him, causing Pauline to arch her back in the beginnings of the dance of sexual intercourse. "Put your head just here," he said, indicating the thigh of his bent leg, "and let me put my head on your so beautiful leg as well. Let us taste of each other the nectar I so desire."

With a low chortle in her throat, Pauline obliged, bending her leg so as to let him rest his blonde head on her own bent thigh, putting his nose but mere inches from the hairy mound that covered her creaming snatch.

In perfect rhythm they nuzzled and tongued each other, he thrusting his nose, then his pointed tongue into her vagina, open to the utmost for him. With his thumb he massaged her tender clitoris, causing her gyrations to become more and more wild, as she waited for him to fill her. She took his penis gently into her mouth, commencing to suck him in and out, in and out, until he was writhing in such ecstasy she feared he would come before she could take him properly into herself.

14

She withdrew her mouth from his now enormous erection, flipping herself around and under him. He took the message. Raising himself on his elbows, placing his legs inside her wide stretched thighs, Leclerc slowly and deliberately sunk the length and breadth of his hard on into her hot interior, a centimeter at a time, bringing her to higher and ever higher planes of desire. Thrusting slowly then withdrawing, thrusting a tiny bit farther, then again withdrawing, had her clutching him in a viselike grip, clawing at his back in her agony of unfulfilled desire. At last he took pity, and thrust himself home, once, twice, three times. It was enough. Pauline howled in unfettered pleasure, twitching and thrusting in one gigantic, totally satisfying orgasm. A moment later Leclerc uttered a mighty groan and shot his sperm up in to the warm and so welcoming vagina of his lady.

From the nearby quarters, Odette put her hands over her ears, the better to keep out the almost animal sounds of pleasure emanating from the main cabin. She prayed the lovemaking was over, at least for the night, but was thwarted in her desire. From her count, the General and his lady pleasured each other at least three times more throughout the long night as *L'Ocean* ploughed its way eastward toward the Caribbean and their final destination.

With her own experience of unfulfilled sexual activity with Boucher, she wondered just what she was missing. But some of the lovemaking of her mistress and her husband sounded so painful, perhaps she did not want to find out.

The ship sailed steadily on through league after league of open ocean, drawing nearer and ever nearer to San Dominguc and the prospect of heavy fighting. Pauline began to become more and more bored, as her husband found it necessary to spend most of every day, and often far into the night, with his staff officers. He was unable to meet her insatiable sexual demands, and she started flirting with some of his junior officers and even a few of the more handsome sailors on board. Odette, well used to her mistress's foibles, shut her eyes and kept her own counsel, telling no one of some of the things she had seen and heard.

One day she was in the passage leading to the cabins of the Leclerc party, when she heard a low chortle coming from an alcove used to store some extra baggage. Passing the door, Odette saw a burly sailor, trousers down around his ankles, leaning back against the wall, thrusting his hips forward at a woman who kneeled at his feet. From the groans and thrusting hips of the man, Odette knew someone was giving him a blow job. She was about to berate this unknown female; how dare she enter the private quarters and pursue her little amours on what was the doorstep of the Leclercs' cabin? But Odette paused before speaking. Somehow the back of the woman's head was familiar, as was the filmy shawl, bordered with a band of classic Greek key design. It was Pauline who was down on her knees, giving pleasure to one of the common sailors, with no thought of being apprehended in her labors. For laboring she was, puffing and panting as the huge schlong of the man slid rhythmically in and out of Pauline's open mouth, giving off loud sucking sounds as it went. Odette turned quietly in the narrow corridor and fled back up the companionway and to the after deck, where she grabbed up a bit of mending she had been working on and bent her head over her needle. Scarlet faced, she drew in deep gulps of balmy sea air to slow her pounding heart.

By the time Pauline strolled casually out on deck, some fifteen minutes later, Odette had gained her composure, but she found it hard to even look into the face of the woman who had been, so shortly before, kneeling before a man who was not her husband, his sperm about to shoot forth into her mouth and down her throat. Odette felt sick, even thinking about the scene she had just witnessed. How could Pauline have been so lewd? But why was she sparkling with sexual fulfillment now, why had she so enjoyed her nibble on a part of the male anatomy Odette found truly distasteful? Was there another way of looking about what she, Odette, considered her duty toward her husband? Was there much she could learn?

At last the endless six week voyage came to an end, and the flotilla sailed past the windward side of Hispaniola and rounded the western end, coming to a halt in the bay at Le Cap. The endless, restless motion of the ship had finally stopped, and it rode gently at anchor in the still waters, protected by the hills ringing the harbor.

Chapter Two

Arrival In Hispaniola

Lookouts for the Generals of this revolution on this Caribbean Island had been watching for several weeks for the arrival of Napoleon's flotilla, which now was spread out before them, mighty and strong. However, neither Toussaint L'Ouverture nor his first General, Henri Christophe, was about to give up.

L'Ouverture sent a fast runner to his underling with the message that, if the French started firing on the town, he was to burn it to the ground, rather than let the French land and establish themselves on the island. The strength of the rebels was far inferior to the troops sent by Napoleon, but they had the advantage of intimate knowledge of their island home, and were well trained in the art of guerilla warfare as well.

According to Napoleon's orders, Leclerc was to try diplomacy first before any fighting commenced. Hence, the morning after their arrival, the General mustered his staff and, in their best uniforms and under a flag of truce, went ashore to try to negotiate with Christophe.

The ladies were left onboard, with no idea when they would again be able to set foot on terra firma.

Pauline lounged under an awning set up for her comfort on the after deck, watching her husband and his entourage being rowed to shore. She wore the flimsiest of muslin dresses, and it was questionable if she wore anything at all under it, so hot and humid was it in the harbor with the ship at anchor. Dermide played with some tin soldiers at her feet, his nanny, Mme duBois, crouched over the game, ready at a moment's notice to join in or take him entirely away, should he start to whine and disturb his mother.

Pauline fanned herself languidly, casting glances over at one of the younger officers guarding the gangway, hot and sweaty under the splendor of his uniform.

Odette had her traveling desk balanced in her lap, waiting for the letter Pauline wished to dictate to Napoleon, telling him of their safe arrival. The lady in waiting gazed around her, fascinated at these first glimpses of the island on which she had been born. She had left as a small child in 1887, to accompany her father to France where he had a minor post in the court of Louis XVI and Marie Antoinette.

From her divan, Pauline abruptly began her dictation, which Odette had to hurry to dip her pen and follow the sometimes confusing prose of her mistress.

"Tell my dear brother," began Pauline, "that we had an absolutely horrible voyage; that I was sick throughout the entire crossing and it is only by the absolutely greatest luck that I arrived here alive." She paused, as if to collect her thoughts.

Odette wrote as fast as she could, noting that – according to Pauline – no one else in their party had been ill at all; all was focused on her.

Tell him I send my most loving greetings, that we will do our best to do our bidding while on this God-forsaken island. That I expect my health to further deteriorate in the terrible heat and humidity...." she paused again.

"Oh! And the bugs. Make sure to tell him of the bugs."

The ship's bell began to ring, and the women paused to count the strokes. It bonged eight times, signifying that the time was noon and the forenoon watch was at an end.

Pauline perked up immensely, as the officer she had spotted earlier prepared to turn over the watch of the companionway to his relief.

"Quickly," she said to Odette. "Go over and ask that Lieutenant to come over here. I wish to speak to him."

Odette knew what was coming, but rose without protest and went over to the companionway.

"Lieutenant, Mme. Leclerc wishes to address you. Please follow me."

The officer saluted his replacement and hastened to obey Odette's obvious command.

He bowed before Pauline, who gave him a hand to kiss, letting her short puffed sleeve fall over her shoulder, giving the man an even better view of her breast, barely covered as it was with the thin material of her bodice.

"It is Lieutenant Soule, is it not?"

"How kind Madame is to remember my name."

"You looked so hot and uncomfortable, standing there in the sun for so long. Please accompany me to my cabin for a cool draught of wine. You finish the letter to my brother," she ordered Odette. "You know what to say to him."

Blushing to the roots of his hair, the young man could but stammer, "Madame is too kind." He helped her to her feet and gave him an arm to lead her below, which she grasped gratefully and leaned against him provocatively. Behind them, on the deck, a couple of sailors gave the universal symbol for what was obviously coming.

Paulette paid no heed. Head practically on the Lieutenant's shoulder, supported by his strong arm, she ducked down the companionway and disappeared into the gloom, the young man only inches behind her. With her husband ashore trying to negotiate with the rebel forces, Pauline knew she had a good few hours for dalliance, and the young man looked to be a wonderful companion for such pleasures. It was well known that Pauline only favored men with big pricks; the

20

bulge she had noticed in this one's trousers the last time she had flirted with him made him a likely candidate. If she was disappointed, what matter? The ship was full of randy men and all of those men had penises, big, small, indifferent. Pauline intended to sample only the best of them.

Odette resumed her place on deck and gazed at the town, spread out before her around the bay and climbing up behind into the foothills that, in turn, led up to the blue mountains beyond. Home lay somewhere up there, the home she hoped to see – after so many years' absence – in a few days time. All would depend, of course, on the negotiations going on at this moment ashore.

Sighing a little, she turned to the letter and the instructions of Odette. It was well known that her mistress had received the very vaguest of formal schooling. Pauline could write, after a fashion, but her knowledge of both grammar and spelling were appalling, and Odette had to recopy each and every letter dictated to her before sending off. It would not do for such missives as Pauline dictated go off verbatim. Odette's early convent education, later, the lessons she had received from her Aunt, stood her well in her present position.

She was writing away, so intent on her task she failed to notice one of the boats returning from shore. She heard the commotion at the gangplank, the presentation of swords, click of heels, and looked up to see yet another young Lieutenant coming over the side. He strode over to stand in front of her, removing his uniform hat as he did so, and executed a small bow.

"Mme. Boucher?"

"Yes," said Odette, looking up at the young man. Dark locks framed a square face, honest and open. He had large gray eyes and his skin had darkened considerably from the time spent at sea, giving him a healthy glow. His firm chin framed a too wide mouth, which was now showing straight white teeth in a smile as he gazed down at her.

"Lieutenant Duval at your service. I have a message for Mme. Leclerc which her husband wishes delivered immediately."

"Mme. is indisposed at the moment," Odette murmured, playing for time. "Perhaps if you would give me the General's message and I can relay it to her as soon as possible?

I am sorry," the young man said firmly. "The General said she must be interrupted whatever she is doing. The message is of utmost importance."

Odette arose most reluctantly. "Then I will go to her," she said. "And bring her to you immediately." She did not relish her task, but saw no way to circumvent it. "If you will wait here, please."

The Lieutenant clicked his heels and gave a slight bow. "Of course, Madame. Thank you."

Odette descended to the shadowy companionway leading to the cabins of the Leclercs, the child and her own small quarters. Through the slatted door at the end she could hear unmistakable sounds of lovemaking. How embarrassing to break in on her mistress, obviously in flagrante delicto with the young Soule.

She knocked, softly at first, then with more firmness. There was no reply from inside, from where squeals and slaps were emanating. With no other recourse, Odette pushed open the door an inch or two and peered around the frame.

The young man was down on all fours, prancing around the floor like a child's hobby horse. On his back, stark naked, rode Paulette, a crop in hand. She was alternately squealing and applying the whip to the man's exposed buttocks, which showed red stripes where she had plied the leather. He sported an enormous hard on, almost reaching the floor and the couple was making so much noise that neither heard Odette enter the cabin. A couple of polite clearings of the throat brought no cessation to the sex play, so Odette was forced to cross the floor and stand beside the besotted couple.

"Madame," she began, raising her voice and putting her foot plainly in Odette's line of vision. "Madame, I am so sorry to interrupt you, but an urgent message from your husband has just arrived and he insisted you hear it immediately."

22

The man stopped his antics and paused, uncertain what to do. Pauline did not turn a hair. "What is this message?"

"There is an officer on deck waiting to give it to you."

"Then leave me long enough to dress and I will join you on deck." She stood up, breasts bouncing enticingly, crop still in hand. "Now leave me."

Odette could but back out of the room, though as she did so she saw Pauline drag the young man up from his position on the floor, push him into the bunk, and mount him hungrily, bouncing away as she rode him eagerly to her own finish line. As she shut the door, the lady in waiting heard the animal sounds coming from Pauline's throat she had heard so often before, both while her mistress was fucking her husband and the number of other men on whom she had bestowed her favors.

Odette was scarlet faced as she returned to Lieutenant Duval. From beneath them came the sounds of wet sucking as Pauline brought Soule to screaming, satisfying orgasm.

"Madame is dressing. She was – uh – resting and will be with you in a few moments." She turned to go over to the side and gaze landward toward the lovely town of LeCap.

Duval joined her, as scarlet faced as she. "May I point out some of the interesting points of the town?" he asked.

"Please do. I was born here but left as a small child," she told him. "I really don't remember much at all about the town so would like to know what some of the buildings are."

Slowly, they came back to normal and managed to look at each other as Duval pointed out the Presidential Palace, which Christophe used as his headquarters, the theaters and the street of fancy shops, which catered to the wealthy planters who came into the town from their estates on the surrounding hillside.

By the time Odette appeared, a scant quarter of an hour later, both Odette and Duval were composed enough to turn and face her, their faces passive once again.

"Yes," Pauline demanded imperiously. Odette noticed that Soule had not accompanied her on deck, and that her mistress was clad in the scantiest of peignoirs, which was obviously all she wore.

"Your husband had commanded me to tell you that the negotiations are not going well, and he does not expect that you will be joining him onshore. He asks you be prepared to have the ship sail away should this prove necessary, you and the child and your suite. He indicated Odette and the hovering lady's maid with one well formed hand, sprinkled across the back with silky dark hairs.

"Is that all?"

"Yes, Madame."

"Then go back and tell my husband I have received his message and will act on his instructions if necessary." Pauline turned on her heel and vanished below decks again.

"I take my leave, Madame," Duval said, taking Odette's hand and kissing it again. "And I hope we will meet again...soon."

'I hope so, too," said Odette softly. She watched him leave the ship, slip down the rope ladder to the waiting boat, and be rowed again toward shore. And stood there for a long time after she could no longer see his dark head bobbing in the prow of the small craft.

The women waited anxiously onboard, hoping for a further message from Leclerc regarding the negotiations with Christophe on shore, but none was forthcoming. Late in the afternoon the boats took off from the pier, heading across the still water back to *L'Ocean.* Even Pauline was topside, holding her small son by the hand. Leclerc swung himself up over the side, to the accompaniment of the pipes of the marine band shrilling his arrival. He saluted the officer of the day and strode up to the afterdeck where his wife waited anxiously with Odette and Marie Claire in attendance.

"Damn the renegade!" he exclaimed. "He has refused any diplomatic resolution to this problem and says he will never surrender."

Pauline made a moue of distaste. "So we are stuck on this god forsaken ship," she exclaimed. "Will I never have my feet on firm ground again?"

Clearly Leclerc was not in the mood to placate her. "Yes, but it is more than that. I will have to lead an expedition inland to take the town from the rear. I could, of course, train our guns on it, but that would result in retaliation which would put you and all the squadron in danger." He indicated the companion boats, bobbing at their own anchors, all around the harbor. "This way, if he fights, he will train his own guns inland, thus keeping all of you safe." He looked exhausted, and Odette hoped Pauline would take him down to the cabin for rest and refreshment, not another round of rollicking sex. One never knew with Pauline.. Almost always her own needs came before anyone else's, regardless of the consequences.

"Surely you need a respite," Pauline cooed, taking her husband's arm and rubbing against his side. "Come with me and I will see that you we are not disturbed this hour. You have had enough for one day, surely, of military matters." She gazed up into her husband's eyes, her tongue flickering over her lower lip. "Take Dermide and entertain him," she told the child's governess, Mme. duBois.

"As you wish, Madame." The woman took the child's hand and led him over to the side of the ship, pointing out various landmarks on shore to the child.

Pauline took Leclerc's arm and led him below to their cabin. Very soon the unmistakable sounds of their lovemaking drifted back up the companionway to those still on the afterdeck. Odette sighed; as always, her mistress was true to form.

Leclerc had no other option but to gather a force to scale the hills beyond the town and attack Christophe from his stronghold of LeCap itself. He was unaware of Toussaint L'Ouverture's words to his Lieutenants when the French fleet was sighted off the shores of the island. "We are doomed," he announced. "All France has come to Saint-Dominigue." His only strategy was to order Christophe to burn the town to the ground, sending its inhabitants up into the hills for shelter. He and his army would camp out in the impregnable jungle, leaving the French to occupy the coast. He hoped that, with fever season approaching, this scourge would wipe out most of the invading force, leaving the island again to him and his minions. His hopes would not be realized.

Messages went out to various captains of the French fleet to prepare their soldiers for an attack on the rebels; such attack would begin a day hence under cover of darkness. All that day there was much activity on shipboard as the troops were readied, and many boats swiftly rowed from the fleet's flagship to the other vessels surrounding it. Finally, as dusk was falling, flotillas of boats was lowered, each filled to capacity with fully armed soldiers and the raid on the island commenced.

Pauline and Odette hung over the side, watching as each boat pulled away. Leclerc was in one of the first to depart, and would await his soldiers on shore nine leagues to the west of the town of LeCap. Boucher and Duval were in charge of two divisions, and Odette's heart went out more to the Lieutenant than to her own husband.

Finally, several hours later, all the boats had departed, and the first of them had started on their return journeys. There was nothing to do but wait with as good grace as possible.

For once Pauline did not seem to be looking for a burly sailor with whom to while away an hour or two. She invited Odette and Mme. duBois to take supper with her, after which they played a desultory game or two of faro, the game banned during the French Revolution which had regained popularity during the Directoire and Consulship. Pauline played the banker, flipping over each card with dexterity and collecting the money waged by each of the other two ladies. They drank wine, which had been cooled somewhat in buckets of sea water and managed for an hour or two to forget what was going on ashore. The night was muggy and the ladies were dressed in their sheerest gowns, with Pauline lolling on her divan in a diaphanous dressing gown, which slipped from time to time revealing a rounded breast or naked leg.

At midnight Pauline yawned and sent the other two off to their quarters. Odette hoped this was one night her mistress would spend alone, but no. Almost as soon as she was ushered out she heard the unmistakable tread of heavy shoes in the companionway and managed to peek out, unobserved. There was the sailor from a couple of days ago, the one whose penis was inserted into Pauline's mouth, thrusting and jerking in his orgasm while Pauline played it like a piccolo. It was rumored around the ship that Mme. Leclerc only fucked those who were well endowed, and that she checked prospective bedfellows out first by performing fellatio on them.

Pauline could but believe it was true, though she had no such yardstick to measure her own husband's erection. She had gone straight from the convent to marriage, and the hasty couplings only underscored her distaste for the act of intercourse between a man and a woman. Boucher's erection was short and stubby and gave no pleasure to his wife, the few times he deigned to thrust it into her unwilling vagina. The thought flitted across her mind that perhaps Duval had a different kind of penis, one that, when inserted into that dark place between her legs would bring some pleasure. Certainly Pauline must enjoy her couplings; she did so often enough, sometimes almost under the nose of her husband. The game of love must be more complicated than Odette realized. She sighed, and lay down to try to sleep through the noises that were even now emanating from the cabin just next door to her sleeping quarters.

On shore the raiding party landed many hours after departure from the harbor, and was having a terrible time in the dark, trying to scale the hills behind the town when they could not see where they were going or what they were doing. Leclerc ordered a rest after a couple of hours of this tortuous raid, instructing that they would continue toward the town at first light. They were almost 50 miles removed from their destination, and forced to march in heavy French field uniforms through

27

extremely rugged and utterly unknown terrain, through hills and tropical forests. Indeed, many of their number collapsed in the unaccustomed heat and humidity and when they finally reached their goal and came to the top of the hills sloping down to Le Cap, their worst fears were realized. Immense clouds of red smoke billowed above Le Cap, seeming to reach to the heavens. For General Christophe, acting on the orders from his superior, L'Ouverture, had indeed burned the entire town to the ground, leaving nothing but smoking rubble. This inferno had impacted many of the ships of the French fleet, which had been close to shore and were in great danger of catching fire and consuming all on board. Fortunately, they had managed to move farther offshore, though some were actually scorched in the process, so high were the flames and scorching heat of the burning town. This conflagration was so intense that it burned for three solid days.

Leclerc and his troops could but watch helplessly from the hills. The French engaged Christophe in battle, and gained the advantage, though losing 500 soldiers in the process. Eventually they returned to their various ships to plan the next stage of their campaign.

Nothing daunted, Leclerc again tried diplomacy. He sent L'Ouverture's two sons to him at his home on the west coast at Ennery. These sons had been educated in France and had traveled out to their native land on one of the ships of the French fleet. They were accompanied by their tutor and a letter from Leclerc, begging him to surrender his power to the new French government of the island. L'Ouverture did not reply.

Leclerc then issued proclamations, both from himself and from Napoleon. Basically the citizens of San-Domingue were promised they would retain their freedom, stating that neither he nor Napoleon wished to reinstate slavery, though this would prove untrue in the long run. Leclerc stated this promise would be faithfully obeyed, and that to do otherwise would be a crime.

Leclerc moved at will around the colony, though with the Presidential Palace burned with all the town, there seemed to be no place on shore for his wife and her attendants. They were stuck on the ship, a situation which pleased no one least of all Pauline.

It was here that Odette came to the rescue. Her family's plantation, La Colline Verte, had occupied a position on the foothills behind the town of LeCap, and she requested a party venture out to see if it was still in habitable condition. She had been in correspondence with the major domo there, still employed by her to keep order, and, as of sailing from France, Odette had been assured that all was in condition for her to occupy the house at her convenience. She only prayed that the fire which had consumed the town had not spread to the surrounding hills, but there was only one way to find out.

Seeing a possible solution to the problems of housing his family and staff officers on shore, Leclerc was only too happy to send a party to see if the house and surrounding grounds had survived. Duval, formerly a lieutenant, now a major due to his bravery during the march to Le Cap, was delegated to take a party to La Colline Verte and vet it for suitability for a residence.

Odette was forced to wait with such patience as she could muster, for the report on her former home. It was not long in coming.

On a brilliant February morning, the temperature hovered at 80 degrees, not so different from home in June. But the humidity was dangerously high, even at an early hour, and those on board were feeling it keenly.

A boat approached *L'Ocean* from the land side and came to rest just below the ladder leading up to midships from the water. Major Duval swung smartly over the side, and strode to the afterdeck where Pauline was reclining on a divan, the others grouped around her.

"Mme. Leclerc," the officer announced, "Mme. Boucher. I am happy to let you know that your home, Mme. Boucher, is in perfect shape, thanks to the careful attention of your major domo, who has spared no trouble all these years to keep everything in readiness for your arrival home."

"Bless Jacques," exclaimed Odette. "My mother was most fond of him as I remember. He must be an old man now, with so many years in the service of my family."

"Old perhaps," said Duval, "but in perfect health, both mind and body. He has done an amazing job and is awaiting you even now to welcome you to your childhood home." He raised Odette's hand to his lips, lingering just a moment too long perhaps, but in that moment he gazed deeply into her eyes imparting a sense of impending excitement that was not lost on the sharp gaze of Pauline. So her little companion might now find a love of her own, eschewing the not so tender attentions of her dolt of a husband. Well, it was about time. Pauline intended to watch this little romance play out to its inevitable conclusion. It would add some spice to her days in which her own husband more often than not was out and about on the business of the First Consul. And even she could not make love every hour of every day.

"Tell us about the trip to the plantation, and what it will be like for us there." She settled back to hear the story.

Duval had ridden out at the head of a column of fifteen handpicked soldiers to inspect the plantation where, hopefully, the General, his lady and their suite could reside while the town was rebuilt. He had no great expectations that there would even be a plantation house standing, or that it would be suitable for a governor's mansion, however temporary. The column had cantered around the town, still smoldering in places from the recent fire, until they came out onto a broad savannah sweeping back from the bay to the high blue mountains in the distance. It was a typical sunny morning on the island, hot and humid so that even at an early hour both the men and their horses had begun to sweat. Flies and other biting insects – a scourge of these tropical shores – rose in clouds around them and, from the sparse trees along the path tropical birds trilled and shrilled their songs to the skies. Brilliant flowers draped themselves over trees and bushes, splashes of vivid color amidst the green of the plain. Ahead were shady places where the jungle was taking over, dark and forbidding with unknown dangers lurking. The low hanging trees and vines could well have hidden a large number of Christophe's men but, thankfully, the French soldiers arrived at the gates of La Colline Verte without incident. The gates stood hospitably open, leading to a drive of crushed seashells which stretched through a stand of acacia trees leading up to an imposing structure of large proportions.

Duval's second in command reigned in beside him. "I guess Boucher will be happy seeing the size of his wife's dowry," he commented to his superior.

"None of our business," Duval replied curtly, spurring his horse to a canter up the drive and arriving first at the long, wide verandah which enclosed three sides of the house with its shade. French doors opened into the house proper and a second balcony wrapped itself around many of the upstairs rooms. It looked to be in good repair, surprising on this island which had seen such recent upheaval. It hardly seemed possible.

Duval dismounted, tying his mount to one of the railings and, without waiting for his escort, mounted the steps and crossed the verandah.

The sturdy front door opened before him, and a man was revealed within the depths of the hall.

It was an elderly mulatto, impeccably dressed in a butler's striped vest, bowing before him.

"Bonjour, Monsieur. You are from the French fleet in the harbor?" He held the door open for Duval to cross before him into the shadows of the hall which stretched the width of the house, from the front verandah to a lush tropical garden out back.

Duval hesitated but for a moment. Surely this was not a trap, especially as the butler could see the other soldiers filing up the drive toward the house. He decided to throw caution to the winds and entered the house.

The hall was wide, with two or three chambers opening off each side. In the dim light it was hard to see much, but Duval noticed the shape of furniture here and there: a pier table inside the door, a rattan chair through an open door, shelves full of books. It must be the library of the house.

He heard boots on the verandah and retraced his steps to the front door, meeting his soldiers as they dismounted.

"All seems to be in order here," he announced. "There is actually a major domo who seems to come with the house." He turned to the black man, who had followed him back down the hall.

"Jacques at your service, gentlemen," the man announced.

"Jacques, then. He was just showing me over the establishment. Surround the perimeter. Notify me if there is any disturbance." He turned and again followed the major domo through the house.

There were six reception rooms on the ground floor, quite suitable for an army headquarters for Leclerc and his immediate staff. The ladies could even use the small parlor at the back, and there was, of course, the verandah, where he visualized Pauline, Odette and their entourage spending much of their time. There was a plethora of comfortable chairs, and even a hammock slung in one corner, with a trellis of violent purple bouganvilla shading it from the heat of the sun. Upstairs were six corresponding bedrooms, each large and airy, all opening to the upper verandah to maximize any breeze from either the harbor below or the mountains behind. Much of the furniture was worn, though all was clean. In any case, Paulette had brought along hundreds of meters of material with which to cover chairs and sofas and divans which she had expected to find in the Presidential Palace in the town. Now they could do duty for this well placed manor which, fortunately, was still standing.

From the back of the house stretched away acres and acres of sugar cane, still being worked by a much reduced force of former slaves. The major domo had managed to keep the sugar cane production going all the while the house owners had been in France, first sending the produce on ships to Europe. Now, with the former slaves in control of the island, much of the cane, which had given the island its great prosperity, was rotting in the fields, with nowhere to go and no place to garner money for the rebels.

Inspection completed, Duval mustered only a few of the troops, leaving the rest behind to guard the property while he rode down to the harbor, took ship for *L'Ocean* to make his report, either to Leclerc if he was on board, or to Pauline and Odette if he was not. He had found the ladies alone, awaiting news of the expedition, and made haste to report to Odette and Pauline. Mme. Leclerc thanked him prettily for his efforts.

She rose from her comfortable divan. "Tiens," she announced. "Let us go as soon as possible. I cannot get off this dratted ship one moment too soon. I can hardly wait to see your former home, Odette. I am sure we will all be very comfortable there." She turned to Duval. "Send word to my husband that we will be repairing to La Colline Verte just as soon as possible. We can always take enough for a few days and send for the trunks later. I assume it is safe for us to be up in the hills?"

"Yes, the rebels have pretty much scattered," Duval told her. "And I will be in charge of the troops guarding the residence of Madame and of General Leclerc. Rest assured of that."

"Oh, I am quite assured of our safety," Pauline told him. "Especially as it will be you in charge of it." She led the way down to the companionway, calling for her maid as she went. The sooner she got off the boat the better she would feel. Even the gentle motion in the harbor made her feel queasy; thank goodness soon she would be on terra firma and in a real house, not these ship's quarters, however opulent they might be.

Odette happily followed her mistress. Soon, oh, so soon, she would see her old home again and the faithful major domo who had kept it going for her all these years.

Chapter Three

At La Colline Verte

The carriages pulled up to the verandah of La Colline Verte mid morning a couple of days later. It had taken that long for Pauline to organize her mountains of baggage, which included beds, linens and a bathtub where Pauline intended to soak and soak and soak an afternoon away after the extremely limited bathing facilities on board ship. Odette had far less baggage and far more personal interest in the house they would be occupying, but she was forced to remain with her mistress and her frantic rooting through the scores of trunks and bundles with which she had crossed an ocean. Finally, on the third morning, all was ready and a short line of hastily rounded up carriages from some of the neighboring plantations that had survived the burning of the town had been commandeered for the journey up into the hills.

Pauline was handed into the first such conveyance, a landeau with two chestnut horses tossing their heads, ready to go, by her husband. She landed on the somewhat fusty cushions with a squeal, and immediately put up her parasol against the rays of the sun, which were even now pounding the island with a hot and humid fist. Odette followed, her husband grudgingly handing her up beside Pauline. He was anxious to go on campaign again, wipe out any pockets of insurrection which smoldered all over the island, threatening the safety of all the French who had landed so shortly ago on these shores. He swung onto his horse and, beside Leclerc, they escorted the open landau around the outskirts of the town and up the bumpy road to the highlands where their destination lay.

Odette gazed around wide eyed, viewing her native land with much interest. Beside her Pauline complained about the inferiority of the carriage and the humidity and heat which brought clouds of stinging insects down on them as they climbed above the town to the fertile land above.

"Phew," she exclaimed. "What torture being here. I am expiring from the heat and even now I am dripping wet. Just look at my dress! It is clinging to my legs."

"Your legs, my dear," Leclerc observed dryly. "There seems to be nothing under your dress to hold the damp cloth away from them. Perhaps a petticoat might have been in order?"

"And make me even hotter?" retorted Pauline. "I think not." She fanned herself vigorously, which did little to dispel the torpid air.

They continued on in silence, passing cane fields wherein labored dozens of black workers, men, women and children, each performing a different task. The men whacked at the tough cane stalks with their huge machetes, the women collected the downed stalks and the children piled them into pyramids at the end of each row, to be collected by an open wagon pulled by four sturdy horses.

"See how your people labor on your behalf," Boucher commented to Odette. "Surely the proceeds from all this will only swell my coffers."

"As you say," murmured Odette politely. That this land had come with her when she married Boucher had certainly been a factor in his pursuit of her. When the French overcame the former slaves who were now working for small wages, the income realized from their labor should be considerable. Boucher gave Odette an almost fond glance, which she pretended not to notice.

Jacques was waiting on the verandah and hastened down the steps when the carriages pulled up. His face was almost split in a grin of welcome and he held out both hands in greeting.

"Mme. Leclerc, welcome. I hope you will be happy here in this house." He gave a small bow as he helped her from the carriage, before turning to Odette. "And Mme. Boucher! I would have recognized you anywhere, though I have not seen you in so many years! You will see from the portrait in the salon just how much you look like your sainted mother." He gave another bow before helping his new mistress out and handing her up the shallow steps to the veranda, where Pauline impatiently tapped her foot.

"It has been tiring traveling up here," she said, though the trip had been no more than three quarters of an hour. "I would like to see our quarters. I trust the beds and bedding have arrived and have been put together?" She turned to leer at her husband over her shoulder, a gaze that was not lost on anyone present.

"Indeed, Madame, your wishes have been carried out to the best of my abilities. I have taken the liberty of engaging a few house servants, to be approved by you, of course."

"Of course," Pauline told him. "You take care of this, Odette." She gestured for Leclerc to join her and together they followed Jacques into the house and up the staircase to the second floor.

On the veranda Boucher offered his arm to Odette. "We too should go up and – uh – view our own quarters. I expect to be off with the General fairly soon so we should take advantage of this time together."

"Indeed," murmured Odette, knowing what was coming. Pauline would draw Leclerc into a long afternoon of violent and noisy love making and no doubt Boucher would take her as well, in his quick and expedient fashion, leaving her damp and unsatisfied. It was his right as her husband to use her in this fashion, and she knew no way of gainsaying him. Sighing, she went with him into the hall and up the stairs after Pauline and Leclerc.

At the top of the stairs, Pauline darted, giggling, into the biggest chamber, pulling an uncomplaining Leclerc after her. The door shut with a bang. Jacques, unperturbed, ushered the Bouchers into the room across the hall, the one which had been occupied by Odette as a small child. Here was a double bed, swathed in the necessary mosquito net, a wardrobe and candle stand, and a long lounge chair under the French doors which opened onto the upstairs balcony. Various trunks and bundles were scattered around the room and a young black maid was starting to unpack.

"Leave us," commanded Boucher imperiously and the girl dropped a quick curtsey and scurried out of the room after Jacques, who shut the door behind him more gently than the one across the hall had been slammed but a moment before.

Odette stood quietly by the bed, waiting for her husband to make the first move – as always. He was striding around the room, flicking his riding crop at a trunk here, at the wardrobe there, testing the handles on the French doors. She screwed up her courage to speak.

"It seems that Mme. Pauline and General Leclerc spend more time in – uh – congress when they are together," she began hesitantly. "Perhaps he makes Madame feel more desired than you do me." There! She had said it and there was no taking it back. Already the two could hear unmistakable sounds of delight emanating from across the hall.

Boucher turned to her, his face scarlet. "You do not expect pleasure from the act of congress," he instructed her. "For you it is merely a preliminary to producing children, which so far you have not managed. Women are the weaker vessel, those who give pleasure and do not expect it in return. You are not a harlot of the docks, expecting voluptuary sensations each time I take you. You are my wife, and I expect you to act accordingly."

"Whatever you say," Odette replied meekly. "You are my husband and I obey you in all things."

"Huh," said Boucher. "I should certainly hope so. Unlike your mistress, who expects pleasure at every turn." He muttered the last almost under his breath and it was all Odette could do to ask why Pauline got to experience pleasure in the sexual act and she should not. It was all very confusing.

Boucher crossed over to the bed and pushed Odette – not ungently – under the mosquito net.　She lay back on the soft muslin coverlet and shut her eyes. Somehow it made it easier if she did not have to see the red faced concentration on her husband's visage each time as he lay above her, pumping away with vigor into her shrinking vagina. It almost made the act impersonal, something to get over as soon as possible.

This afternoon was no exception. Boucher loosened his britches, pushing them down enough so he could mount Odette with ease. He pushed up her thin skirt and petticoat, exposing the loose leg holes of her short pantellettes.　Sometimes he removed this undergarment, making her labia and sweet interior beyond more accessible to his thrusting erection. Today however he merely pushed the flimsy material covering Odette's black bush to one side.　Taking his pulsing penis in his other hand, he guided himself into her dry and scratchy vagina, shoving and grunting in his efforts to thrust his six hard inches in as far as it would go.

Odette shut her lips tight against the pain her husband's hard-on was causing her, praying that he would ejaculate soon and spare her any further pain. Today, however, he seemed to take a perverse pleasure in torturing her by his very slowness, thrusting forward and drawing back with deliberate and measured strokes, not hurrying himself in any way.

Surprisingly Odette realized she had produced some lubrication from deep within her, and the strokes of the rigid penis became almost enjoyable.　Was this what it was all about?　She found her breath was coming harder now, and she caught the rhythm of the sexual act, thrusting her hips higher with each forward thrust from Boucher, trying to measure her movements with him.

He must have sensed her arousal, for Boucher immediately sped up his tempo, thrusting and parrying with such vigor Odette completely lost any participation in this randy intercourse, and instead was thrown and buffeted against the soft mattress. Almost immediately, Boucher gave a loud groan and spurted his pent up sperm into the welcoming warmth of his wife's now slippery vagina, jerking and thrusting one last time in his violent orgasm. He rolled off Odette, turning away from her as he adjusted his trousers, buttoning the sides up over his now limp prick. Odette lay on her back, almost in tears. Had she finally started to understand what could be made of the sex act? Would she ever feel more? She had no idea, but almost reached out to Boucher, hoping for another round. He had already stood up, and was now fully dressed again. He drew her skirt modestly down over the wide parted V or her legs, black muff gleaming up at him. He neither kissed nor caressed her, but simply turned and let himself out of the room. From across the hall the sounds of Leclerc and Pauline had become almost deafening, as Boucher shut the door on his wife and her total lack of satisfaction.

Odette dozed most of the afternoon away under the mosquito net, awakening fully as evening began to fall over the distant blue hills. From the room across the hall there was no sound. Presumably Pauline and Leclerc had finished their wild sexual rompings, leaving the house quiet and – seemingly – at peace. Odette rose from the bed, washed lightly in the tepid water from the ewer and basin placed on a side table, and bound up her hair in one of the jeweled *filets* which had been so popular when they had left France only a few short months before. She donned one of her least wrinkled evening gowns from the large trunk in the corner of the room, and tentatively opened the door.

From Pauline's room came the reassuring sound of soft voices, female. Odette knew this meant that her mistress, too, was dressing for dinner. She tapped gently on the door and waited to be asked to enter.

Pauline was lolling in her portable bathtub which was filled with a rich mixture of milk and water which she demanded daily wherever it was available. Presumably Jacques had sent to the neighboring plantations for as much milk as they could spare, the better to keep Pauline in a good temper. When all her demands – and they were legion

– were met she could be one of the most charming women on earth. Cross her in the smallest matter and she could become, instantly, the worst kind of shrew, shouting and throwing objects across the room. This evening, however, she seemed to be in the most benign of moods, probably due to the long and arduous session of lovemaking with her husband during the afternoon.

Odette dropped a small curtsey and crossed the room to stand beside the tub. Pauline was half submerged in the milky liquid, her famously pert breasts bouncing and floating above the milk and water. She handed her maid a sponge and indicated that the woman was to wash her all over: her back, her neck, her breasts and down to the black bush, visible as a gray mass beneath the bath/milk water. She parted her thighs and lifted her groin toward the sponge, purring gently as the rough surface passed over her tender labia, rendered somewhat red and swollen by all the recent activity of Leclerc's hands and tongue and penis there.

Odette turned modestly away. She knew Pauline would soon give her a description of just how far that love making had gone, and was preparing herself to take the information with equanimity. She did not have long to wait.

"Ah, Odette," her mistress said so softly Odette had to lean closer to make sure she heard properly. "Leclerc was quite a tiger this afternoon! I came close to swooning more than once. Ah, his hands, that probing middle finger in my streaming interior. I made him dip it in sea water first, it is so much more agonizing with all that salt, did you know?" She did not pause for a reply. "I found that out quite by accident when we were forced to bathe in sea water on board the ship. At first I was aghast that no fresh water was available but soon I changed my tune. Mon dieu! What ecstasy! What joy! Le petit morte almost became le grand morte! I truly thought I would die more than once, so intense and so explosive was my orgasm. I should have said orgasms. I can hardly walk for the pleasure I took this afternoon. I may have to be carried down to dinner. I do hope Boucher can pleasure you in the same way my own husband pleasures me. I could go at it all day and all night if only my husband could keep up with me. As it is, I am afraid I wore him out." She gave a little giggle and slid down deeper into the tub. Odette noticed her hand was now under the water and from its rapid motion Odette could tell her mistress was now pleasuring herself. Truly the woman was insatiable!

A few moments later Pauline gave a gasp, shut her eyes and remained still for a few moments, the breasts bobbing gently in the mixture in the tub. Then she opened the eyes, held out her hand and allowed Marie Claire to help her out, sloshing the tub's contents all over the floor as she did so. Her perfect body, unmarked by the birth of Dermide almost three years earlier, was wrapped in a huge linen sheet for the maid to pat her dry. She sat before her dressing table, admiring her reflection in the somewhat smoky mirror set above the mahogany piece and arched her back in cat-like satisfaction.

"Now, what shall I wear for this first gala dinner in your plantation house?" she asked Odette.

"Let me look through the trunks and see," answered Odette.

"Oh, Marie Claire has freshened several of my evening costumes," Pauline said. "They are hung behind that screen." She indicated an elaborate screen in the corner of the room. "Choose from one of them"

Odette found three or four similar muslin and thin lawn gowns, freshly ironed, hung on pegs fastened to the wall. All were practically transparent and cut down so low it would be just about possible to see Pauline nipples through the bodice. If not, Pauline's rouged nipples would certainly be clearly visible through the sheer material. Odette sighed and chose the simplest of the gowns, the better to endure the hot night ahead. In the heat and the torpor of her native land, the heat and the humidity of the island was oppressive for all of the day and much of the night, though there was a brief respite just before dawn when the temperature tended to drop by a few degrees. At other times the white population of the island was fanned by former slaves, now freedmen paid the smallest of wages. These fans were mounted on long poles and were hand waved and of all manner of materials from palmettos to exotic feathers, of huge varieties, mounted in the ceilings and manipulated by ropes pulled by more servants in rhythmic motion while the masters dined, drank or just lounged in the high ceilinged rooms.

Tonight General Leclerc and several of his senior staff were present, along with Pauline and Odette. Once order was more established and planters had returned to their homes around La Colline Verte, Pauline could assume her position as the Governor General's lady and entertain in lavish style. For these first few days they would live simply.

In spite of the heat and the speed with which this household had come into being, Jacques had managed to engage a native cook, together with footmen, housemaids and grooms. He assured Leclerc all of these people were known to him, indeed, had been slaves on the plantation, and were trustworthy. With no other help at hand, Leclerc had found it necessary to take the major domo's word.

The simple evening, therefore, consisted of aperitifs on the verandah, until the swarm of bugs that descended everywhere as night fell drove the company back into the house, where fans helped keep the majority of them at bay. Jacques announced dinner and the ladies were taken in on the arm of their respective spouses, the French officers bringing up the rear.

The long highly polished table was set with service for a dozen. Silver gleamed and napery glistened while low bowls of native flowers: bird of paradise, mimosa and bougainvillea were spaced at intervals along the table.

Odette beamed with pleasure that Jacques had been able to arrange for all this formality in what was her former home, and did not question too closely how he had managed such a feat in such short order. She graciously took her place half way down the table, seated between her husband and Georges Duval, who was detailed to remain behind while the other officers went on maneuvers to guard the women while their respective husbands went out into the island to restore law and order.

Dinner began with a clear turtle soup, made from a native variety that abounded in the waters surrounding the island. With it went a surprisingly good sherry, unearthed from the cellar Odette's father had laid down long ago, before the family sailed for France. Next came a white fish, delicately poached in wine, accompanied by a mousseline sauce, then native pigeon, each bird roasted whole and presented with a mango sauce. An avocado salad was the next and final course of dinner, which was finished off by a sorbet of lemon and lime, accompanied by the thinnest of sugar cookies. This last course produced a conversation amongst the men of the sugar cane production, which had made Napoleon desirous of overtaking the island again for France, and rekindling its rich legacy with its attendant huge revenues. Such agricultural output had been stopped by the slave uprising and subsequent abolishment of slavery by the provisional French government in 1794, which slavery Napoleon wished to re-establish. For this had the great expedition sailed and for this the dozen people were gathered at La Colline Verte to plan how this was best accomplished.

Pauline and Odette withdrew to the small drawing room which had been set aside for their use, while the men gathered around the brandy bottles and the cigars to discuss the topic so dear to men's hearts: war.

Pauline was in a talkative mood.

"Did you see that handsome buck who was serving at the other end of the table?" she blurted out as soon as the women had sat down on the delicate fauteuil's either side of the small fireplace. "He would indeed be a stud worthy of bedding."

"But Pauline," protested Odette. "He is black! Surely you would not consider, I mean...." she stammered, unsure of how to go on.

A gentle cough interrupted her. Jacques was coming through the door, bearing a coffee service on a beautifully polished silver tray.

Odette was sure he had heard the conversation and blushed to the roots of her hair. She did not want to hurt the feelings of this old and faithful servant, who had served her parents and remembered her as a child, no doubt playing in this very room.

Pauline, however, had to such scruples. "Jacques," she demanded imperiously. "Who was that handsome buck serving at dinner this evening?"

An almost indiscernible grimace crossed his face, but he managed to answer in a most polite manner. "He is my nephew, Madame. His name is Zeus."

"How clever!" exclaimed Pauline, "considering the function for which I wish to use him. The general leaves at dawn tomorrow for the interior, with most of his troops. Please have Zeus bring up my morning coffee when I ring. I may need him for – other duties during the morning, so make sure he is not needed elsewhere. You may go." She swept her hand toward the door in an impatient gesture and Jacques bowed and withdrew. Pauline's eyes were sparkling and her red, pointed tongue flickered over her upper lip. She seemed to be in another world for a moment before she came back in spirit to this hot, charming room in the middle of a tropical hillside on a Caribbean island three thousand miles from home.

"Pour the coffee," she instructed Odette, "before it becomes stone cold."

Odette obeyed, her heart sinking in anticipation of what would happen while the General was away.

Early next morning Odette awakened to the familiar sounds from across the hall. Pauline was saying goodbye to her husband in her indomitable fashion. Fortunately, the grunts and moans and slap of bare hand on bare flesh did not last too long. Beside her Boucher slept on, unaware of the violent activity coming from his general's bedchamber. He had come to bed last night fairly drunk and had climbed in beside her, immediately going to sleep. He did not awake until his valet tapped gently on the door the next morning and entered with a steaming pot of coffee and one cup on a tray. Odette made sure she was covered modestly before calling 'enter' and accepted the smallest of kisses from her husband before he climbed from the bed and followed the valet into the next-door tiny chamber which had been designated as a dressing room. Nor did he return to her again before she heard his boots clattering down the stairs, followed almost immediately by a companion pair belonging to Leclerc. She turned over and fell immediately into a deep sleep. She would be spared the attentions of her husband as long as he was away fighting, and that might be a very long time. It would be a time to explore her island home, get to know its people and settle in for the duration, however long that would be.

She awoke much later. The sun was streaming fully through the side windows of her bedchamber, though the light was muted at the front which was shaded by the upstairs verandah. She stretched luxuriously, alone in the wide bed she had shared so recently with her husband.

Odette picked up the bell and rang. She had no idea who would answer, but a few moments later a young black girl tapped at the door and came into the room.

"Yea, Missus," she said softly, in the island patois Odette had not heard since her childhood.

"Coffee, please, and water to wash. What is your name, child."

"I be Jasmine, Missus, like the flower on the porch and in the jungle."

"Jasmine. What a pretty name. Well, Jasmine, I know you will be looking after me very well while I am here. Is Mme Leclerc awake yet?"

The girl looked down at the floor and scuffed her toe along one floorboard.

"Well, Missus, yea, she be up. But in her bath. She call for Zeus."

Another bath! Pauline had just taken one the evening before. And she had asked last night that it be Zeus who took up her morning coffee. Well, that must have been accomplished. Perhaps Pauline was making up for all the salt water she had to endure while on shipboard.

"Well, I had best be up and dressed. Madame may want me soon. Please fetch that coffee then come back and help me."

The girl withdrew, chuckling softly, though Pauline could not figure out why.

She slid out from under the mosquito net, remembering to check inside her satin slippers for any stray bug or other creature that may have taken up refuge there during the night. She opened the French doors to the verandah. She would take a stroll outside and perhaps get a glimpse through the matching doors into Pauline's room; see how far along she was in making her toilette. That way Odette would know how much time she might have before her mistress needed her. She padded softly outside and went around the corner of the verandah where the Leclerc's room was located. She thought to but glance in through the glass, then withdraw. What she saw, however, brought her up short and she found herself riveted to the spot, unable to either look or move away.

Pauline was indeed in her bath, but it was not Marie Claire who was rubbing her with the sponge. Instead it was a tall and powerful black man, clad only in a loin cloth who was performing Pauline's ablutions.

Zeus! The man Pauline had admired last night. Pauline Bonaparte was a law unto herself, everyone knew it. Even her poor husband, Leclerc, who fully expected his wife to be in the arms – and the bed – of other men the moment his back was turned.

Indeed, it had been her propensity for almost continuous sex that had gotten him married to this, the youngest sister of the First Consul, but a few short years ago. He had been waiting for Napoleon in his office, when Pauline had come in looking for her brother. She was only sixteen at the time, a dazzling, petite beauty with dark hair and eyes and the most beautiful breasts – it was said – in all of France. These breasts were practically bursting out of her tight bodice, causing Leclerc to stiffen involuntarily. Pauline had burst out laughing at the bulge in his tight pants, and drawn him behind a screen in the corner of the office. There, to his great surprise, she had unbuttoned his trousers and taken

46

out the engorged penis, stroking and pulling it until Leclerc thought he would burst with desire for this wanton adolescent. She had expertly played him, with fingers and palm, even to the extent of kneeling before him where she took his hard on into her hot, moist mouth, licking and sucking with delighted abandon. As he was about to shoot his pent up sperm into her mouth, unable to contain himself for more than a few more seconds, she had laughed, laid down before him on the cold floor and raised her skirts above her head, giggling as he lunged for her, unable to stop himself, thrusting himself into her willing vagina. It was thus Napoleon found them a moment later, in flagrante delicto, his loyal officer fucking his youngest sister with total abandon. Napoleon's outraged shout did nothing to check Leclerc's ardor, and he shot a huge load of hot, sticky sperm into the willing cunt of this ardent young girl, letting loose an almighty moan as he did so.

Napoleon did the only thing he could under the circumstances. He pried Pauline out from under Leclerc, administered a sharp slap on her bare backside, causing her to cry out in pain, and pulled her skirts down over her nakedness. He sent her off to mope in her room and waited until Leclerc had buttoned his trousers and stood, red-faced before his general, waiting his own punishment. He found not much to his distress, that he would be wedding Pauline as soon as matters could be arranged. Until then he was to return to his regiment and behave. Thus did the union of Pauline and Leclerc come about, a union that was not to prove too unhappy, though Mme Leclerc was never, from day one, faithful to her husband. He had expected no such fidelity, but as his marriage had brought him so close to his mentor and hero, Napoleon, he never complained at the long and varied stream of his wife's lovers. They were married in 1797, when Pauline was sixteen, Leclerc, 24, and produced one son, named Dermide by Napoleon, the following year. There were no more children, and Leclerc's army career was not spectacular until Napoleon chose him as General of the huge French expedition that went to San Domingue in 1802, to put down the slave uprising.

Now, it seemed, Pauline was even at this moment, engaged in a sexual liaison with one of these former slaves. Odette continued to stand – and stare – as her mistress raised herself from the tub, giving her hand to the man who stood with the drying sheet as the maid had done just the previous afternoon. His bulk, next to her small frame, almost engulfed her, and he rubbed and patted through the sheet, almost as one would dry a small child.

Pauline was purring with pleasure as she turned and twisted before the man. She dropped the sheet, standing naked in all her glory. Zeus waited for her instructions. Not for nothing had he been a slave; he expected to be ordered and directed in all things. The fact this rendez-vous with the wife of the French general would, have in earlier days, brought him the most severe beating of his life, if not death, was of no matter now. The black population of this island had been free men and women since 1794, by decree of the French government, and the liberte, egalite and fraternite of all mankind applied as much to him as to this white woman standing before Zeus, even as he waited to see what she would do next. He did not have to wait long.

There was a gigantic bulge in the loin cloth, the only garment worn by Zeus. With practiced fingers, Pauline took one end of the roughly woven flaxen cloth and began to unwind the length of it away from the man's hips and groin. It dropped to the wet floor, sticky with the residue of Pauline's bath, exposing this magnificent specimen of a man in all his glory.

Odette could not stifle an involuntary gasp as this latest conquest of her mistress was revealed in all his glory. Zeus was indeed a perfect name for this incredible specimen of a man. His taut skin, almost the color of fine amber, glowed in the early morning light. Finely muscled calves flowed into a perfectly shaped torso, massive of shoulders tapering to a narrow waist below which a thick triangle of jet black hair supported his incredibly enormous penis, which hung down half way to his knees. As Odette watched, spellbound, Pauline took that massive organ between the palms of her hands, rolling and kneading the length and breadth of it expertly between her palms. It stiffened and hardened, swinging dangerously between the two lovers, pulsing rampantly against Pauline's perfect breasts. She took the swinging meat between these two rounded globes, pushing herself together with her hands, forming a substitute vagina for Zeus to thrust himself into, which he did with gusto. He had not touched her in any way, but Pauline began to sway back and forth in a controlled ecstasy, which became more and more vigorous as the black hard on continued to thrust between her milk white breasts. Somehow the contrast, black skin against white skin made the tableau all the more erotic to Odette's eyes, as she watched her mistress lower her head and take as much of the rampant cock as possible into her panting mouth. Zeus swayed above her, uttering animal sounds of pleasure, head back, groin forward, as he leaned with mounting desire closer to Pauline and her ministrations. She was still in control as she took the man by the hand and led him over to her divan, pushing him back onto the wealth of cushions. She mounted him with satisfaction and lowered herself slowly, ever so slowly onto the pulsing hard on she had created. Moans of pleasure emanated from her throat, which soon were replaced by screams of delight as she rode her stud to a quick orgasm, indeed, her fucking of this magnificent male could probably be heard all over the house. Odette saw Pauline collapse, panting so hard she feared a heart attack, onto the broad amber chest of her lover, lying there for but a few short minutes before she again took the mighty prick in her hand and began to tease and torment it all over again.

Odette managed to step back, tear herself away from the frantic fucking going on before her eyes and, softly she turned and tiptoed her way back around the verandah to her own room. Once there, she felt quite dizzy and lay down on her rumpled bed to recover. The young girl, Jasmine, entered an instant later with the coffee tray and Odette managed to sit up, pour a cup of the steaming brew and take a few sips which revived her. She looked at Jasmine and caught a face devoid of expression. Truly the staff at La Colline Verte had already become accustomed to the General's wife and her sexual romps, both with her husband and, apparently anyone else who struck her fancy.

A half hour later Odette was revived enough to rise and dress. She hoped to ride out over her plantation this morning and went downstairs in search of Jacques, who would surely know the state of the stables down behind the house. She found him in the small 'ladies' parlor' ostensibly dusting the center table. In reality she felt he had been waiting for her. She greeted him pleasantly and sat down in one of the small fauteuils under the window.

"Is there a horse in the stable I might ride? We did not inspect it yesterday and I have no idea as to the number and condition of the mounts," she said to Jacques.

"Indeed yes, Madame," Jacques replied. "The general left suitable mounts for you and Mme. Leclerc, which are being cared for by one of the lads I managed to hire for the purpose. But the general Leclerc insisted that if either of you ladies ride out you must be accompanied. There are still rebels in the hills and there is no knowing how near they may be to the plantation.

"Very well, Jacques," Odette said. "Who will be my escort if I do ride out this morning? I do not know if Mme. Leclerc needs me or not, though I suspect not. Perhaps you would send someone to inquire?" She turned her face away from the Major Domo, embarrassed to think he knew what was going on upstairs and in no way wishing to disturb Pauline in her tryst. Let one of the other servants do so.

"I will go myself, Madame." Jacques bowed slightly and went out of the room and up the stairs.

Odette went over to the marble mantelpiece, more for show than for warmth as there was rarely a fire needed in this tropical climate. A portrait hung on the wall there, of a slender young woman dressed in the fashion of the court of Louis XVI and Marie Antoinette, almost twenty years ago. She was in wide panniered shirts, her hair done elaborately to tower a good two feet over her pale, oval face. Odette studied the visage of the woman who had given her life for her daughter, dead these twenty years. At the start of the Revolution, Odette herself had been spirited away to live with a great aunt in relative obscurity outside of Lyon, only emerging again to join the new society in Paris during the Directoire of Napoleon and his cohorts. She had caught the eye of his sister and become a lady in waiting to her, which position had – strangely enough – brought her here, back to the land of her birth. She was so lost in her reverie she did not hear the return of Jacques, who gave a polite cough to catch her attention.

"Madame will not need you until luncheon," he announced in measured tones. "Perhaps not until this afternoon. She says to enjoy your ride. I will call Colonel Duval, who is head of the troops left behind to guard you and Mme. Le General."

"Call Duval!" Odette asked in surprise.

"Yes, Madame, he received a promotion before the general rode off."

"Thank you, Jacques," said Pauline. "Perhaps you will let the Colonel know I am ready whenever he is also."

"Of course, Madame. May I just say that I remember your mother so well." He indicated the portrait. "And you are so very like her at the same age."

"You remember my birth?" Odette asked in surprise.

"Indeed I do," replied Jacques. "It was twenty years ago this very month your mother brought you into this world. It was a very happy occasion for all of us on this plantation, a new beginning so to speak."

Odette pulled from the neck of her frock a miniature of the portrait over the mantle. "I always wear this," she said, showing it to the Major Domo, "next to my heart. I loved my mother dearly and will always miss her."

""And I, also," said Jacques. Involuntarily his hand went to his throat, a gesture that Odette did not understand at the time. "And now to fetch the Colonel for you, Madame." He bowed and exited the room, leaving Odette to once again turn her gaze to the portrait of her mother.

Duval shortly presented himself, bowing to Odette. "Madame. I understand you wish to ride out. I have been detailed by General Leclerc to accompany you, with a detachment of the troops. We cannot be too careful as there may still be rebels about, hiding somewhere near."

"Of course," murmured Odette. "And may I congratulate you, Colonel, on your promotion."

"I thank you, Madame." Duval bowed again and took up Odette's hand to kiss. Did his lips linger just a bit too long on the back of her hand? Odette could not be sure, but she warmed to this young officer who was now in charge of her safety.

"I will ask the horses be brought around to the verandah," he said.

"Thank you," replied Odette. "Will you take coffee or perhaps a glass of wine while we are waiting?"

"I think not, but thank you. Perhaps when we return?"

"Of course," said Odette. "Perhaps you will stay to luncheon?"

"That would be delightful. Shall we go out to await our mounts?" He offered Odette his arm and escorted her out to the wide verandah. A few moments later two steeds, one gray, carrying a sidesaddle, the other a bay with an army saddle, were led to the front steps. With no mounting block Duval lifted Odette up easily onto her saddle, handling her as if she was but a piece of goose down.

She looked down into his handsome face, burned from exposure to the tropical sun, glints of light gleaming in his dark hair. "Thank you, Colonel," she murmured.

"My pleasure, always, Madame." He swung easily into his own saddle and they started down the drive to the plantation beyond. Behind them a platoon of mounted soldiers fell into formation, swords glittering in the strong morning light.

The walked their horses easily, side by side, down the drive and out into the now fallow fields that had once been the source or enormous amounts of sugar cane on this rich island that had supplied many French aristocrats living abroad with the bulk of their wealth. San Domingue had been the premier island in the Caribbean producing sugar, which production had halted with the abolishment of slavery and now many of the fields were reverting to the jungle from which they had been hacked a century before, while the refining plants, which produced the finished product for export, stood idle, their equipment rusting and useless without the labor of the former slaves of the island. Here at La Colline Verte, however, a major part of the work force had been retained by Jacques and limited production was still underway.

Odette remembered nothing of the plenty of this lush land, which had kept her parents rich for many decades. She did remember, vaguely, the luxury of the life they led in France, however, before the terror had taken her parents to the guillotine and herself to the great aunt who had raised her.

Both Odette and Duval gazed about them with rapture; she because for the first time in her memory she was viewing the land of her birth; he, because he had studied the island and its sugar production prior to coming out with Leclerc's forces. He saw the great natural beauty of the land, abounding with forests on the high mountains, the terraced fields in the lower plains, which had been wrested by slave labor from the jungle which was threatening to encroach once again. He knew that sugar cane depleted the soil and its production was both arduous and long. With unlimited slave labor all that had been possible. Now, with freedom for the blackman he wondered if nature could once again be held at bay and the fields replanted. Surely the intervening fallow period had made the soil rich again, and, if not, then the addition of a large quantity of manure should take care of that. Perhaps once again San Domingue would rise as a premier source for Europe of the much desired refined sugar.

Their route took them around the perimeter of most of the fields, into a small stretch of jungle. Here, under the lush tropical trees, were myriads of wild orchids, growing as parasites among the fronds. Exotic birds trilled and called to each other from treetop to treetop, and a few monkeys, originally brought from Africa by the early slaves scampered high above. From Africa also came many of the exotic fruits associated with the Caribbean: bananas, mangos, pineapples and citrus fruit. Indeed, the jungles of San Domingue resembled a veritable garden of Eden to the eyes of the French who had come to wrest the island from the grip of L'Ouverture and return it to Napoleon and France.

Odette and Duval rode companionably side by side, the troops trailing a discreet distance behind them. From time to time one pointed out to the other some plant or bird of special interest, but for the most part they rode silently, taking in all the beauty around them.

"I wonder," Duval began, "if it would ever be possible to regain the plantation, make it productive again as it was a few years ago?"

"I do not know," said Odette. "I do remember my father discussing how much labor it took to produce the sugar which fueled our life in France. But it was slave labor. If one worker on the plantation died, it was possible to buy a replacement. Or breed one." The last was uttered in a monotone so low Duval had to lean from his saddle the better to hear Odette.

"It sounds like the breeding of dogs," he said, "or sheep."

"I think it was. They – the slaves – were not considered human beings, just animals to serve whatever purpose the master desired: help in the house, labor in the fields. Many a plantation master also used slaves for immoral purposes, the women, I mean. Though I do not think my father ever indulged in such behavior. But on many another plantation there were many children – and adults – who obviously bore both black and white blood in their veins."

"Like Jacques," remarked Duval. "He is very light for a negro."

"He is," said Odette. "He was the product, I believe, of a mulatto slave girl and the master of a plantation near ours. She herself must have been of similar blood."

"And he has run the plantation since your parents left for France? Is that not unusual for a black slave?"

"I understand my mother thought most highly of him," Odette told him. "And taught him herself how to read and write and figure. She said he was one of the most eager for knowledge of anyone she ever knew, and he was a joy to teach. She let him read anything he wanted from the library, hence his store of knowledge."

"And he remained faithful to you and your family throughout the uprising on the island and subsequent abolishment of slavery?

"Yes," said Odette. "Though I am not sure why. He is a freedman now and could pursue any occupation open to him that he wanted. But he has remained loyal to me even though he has not seen me for many years."

"You are aware," Duval said, "that Napoleon wishes to regain control of this island in order to enrich the coffers of France. He would even like to re-impose slavery on the black population here, though how he would accomplish that is not clear. Once a man is free he would never bow again to the bond of slavery, I am sure."

"Perhaps the plantations can be made productive again with paid labor," Odette said. "Though I imagine the profits would be infinitely lower than they were before freedom came."

"No doubt," Duval agreed, 'though now I am here I intend to study just that topic."

Odette gave him a broad smile. "I am so happy that you will do so," she said. "I would be so pleased to see this island become productive again. It is a shame to see so many of these fields lying idle." She gazed out over the broad vista before her, of field after field stretching almost to the horizon, with the blue hills of the island in the far distance.

They cantered up to the verandah hot and sweaty from their ride, just as the sun was positioned overhead, pleased with the new friendship forming between them. Duval handed Odette down from her horse onto the wide steps, letting his hands linger perhaps a moment too long on her slender waist. He took up her hand and bowed over it, allowing his lips gently to brush her knuckles, causing a gentle flutter in Odette's nether parts. She started and drew back. Was this mere politeness on the part of her Colonel, or something more? She did not

55

wish to think on the matter. Turning abruptly, she ran across the verandah and in the front door.

Jacques was waiting for her in the hall. "Madame Leclerc wishes to be excused from luncheon today," he announced. "She will take something in her room. She may even rest there until dinner, so will have no need of you this afternoon. Luncheon will be served in an hour, but in the meantime I have placed some cool wine for you and the Colonel in the small parlor. Will there just be the two of you for luncheon?"

"So it would seem," said Odette with a small smile. "Please send me Jasmine to help me dress." She ran nimbly up the stairs, happier than she had been in some time.

Chapter Four

Maneuvers

With Leclerc and most of his staff away on maneuvers, attempting to wrest control of the island back from the revolutionaries, the household at La Colline Verte was thrown on its own devices for amusement. Pauline chafed at the lack of social events, but had been assured by her husband that as soon as he subdued the island, she would be given her due as First Lady of San Domingue. There were plenty of French citizens still living on their plantations in and around the burned out city of Le Cap. Not only would the general rebuild, he would also ensure his wife was given her proper place as the Governor's Lady. To this end he fought his way through jungles and arid plains, taking back the island for the First Consul, so far away in Paris. The speed with which he and his army moved helped in his cause. By March he had retaken much of the land from the rebels. His biggest triumph would come at the siege of Crete-a-Pierrot.

During this time Pauline and Odette waited anxiously at home, living for the dispatches that Leclerc sent back from the front, brought by speedy messengers over long stretches of terrain. Through much fierce fighting, he was confident of his success.

Odette would read these dispatches to her mistress, who often lounged in the long hammock strung up in a corner of the wide verandah upstairs. It was overhung with swaths of bougainvillea, shading it from the hot, tropical sun for much of the day, cooled slightly from the breezes which wafted up from the harbor far below.

One such morning in March brought a hot and sweaty messenger in on a highly lathered horse. He threw his reins to a waiting groom and ascended to the second story verandah where he bowed before the two women.

"Mme. Leclerc. Mme. Boucher," he panted, striving to catch his breath. "I bring you messages from General Leclerc." He held out a somewhat grubby packet which Odette took thankfully from his fingers.

"Thank you, sergeant," she said. "Please present yourself to the major domo who will arrange for some refreshments, and someplace for you to rest.

"I thank you," said the soldier, who was little more than a boy. He clicked his heels and went back downstairs in search of Jacques.

"Well?" inquired Pauline languidly, "what does my husband say?"

"He is engaging the enemy with all his forces and hopes for victory soon."

"Really," said Pauline, not displaying any interest whatsoever in her husband's news.

In truth she was little interested in what was going on with the army; her only concerns were her own pleasures, which mainly consisted in gently rocking in the hammock on the porch and being serviced by the giant Zeus. She had managed to have his duties transferred to waiting on her exclusively, even to the extent of his sleeping on a pallet outside the French doors from her bedchamber. She had cited this as a necessity in case anyone should try to climb to the second storey and molest her – or, as an afterthought, Odette. She stated that she would feel far safer with her watchdog outside her door, and no one had dared gainsay her command. So the man, completely in Pauline's thrall, was available to her any hour of the day – or night – she chose. And she so chose frequently. Indeed, Odette's duties had been far lessened these last weeks, giving her ample time to ride out with Duval and view her inheritance with him.

Pauline usually managed to rise and dress for dinner, wafting her way downstairs on clouds of Parisian scent, robed in the flimsiest of gowns which did nothing to mask or hide her sexual charms. From her rouged nipples, sometimes popping out the top of her tight bodices, to the lack of any sort of knickers under her skirts, she presented a perfect picture of the totally wanton women she was. That her husband seemed to take no notice of her many amours was put down to his awe of his brother-in-law and his desire to totally emulate him on the battlefield, if not in the bedroom. Napoleon's devotion to Josephine at this time was well known, as was the animosity felt by Pauline for her brother's wife. Perhaps she was jealous that Josephine was first lady of France. At least on this remote island, Pauline occupied a similar position one she fully intended to exploit as soon as her husband was back at her side.

In any event, with Leclerc away, Pauline was getting sex and plenty of it from her hot young stud. At almost any hour of the day and certainly long into the night the occupants of the house at La Colline Verte were treated to all manner of sounds from the upstairs chamber occupied by Pauline. From soft moans and groans to loud, exultant shouts of joy as Pauline or Zeus climaxed, sometimes separately and sometimes together, the household could not but be aware that Pauline's heavy sexual desires were being fulfilled most competently. There was often the slap of a heavy hand on bare flesh, with Pauline shrieking for joy at the corporal punishment bestowed by her lover, as well as the sharper thwacks administered by her with a riding crop on the buttocks of the huge negro. Indeed, these two were so vociferous in their lovemaking that nothing was left to the imagination of those who heard them, who usually went around with red faces, avoiding the gazes of others in the household. Indeed, dinner with the General's lady out of her bedchamber for an hour or two was often the only time of day when such noises were not floating down from the upstairs floor, giving some respite to speculation about the activities above.

Throughout it all Odette wondered: just what was Madame experiencing that gave her so much pleasure, when the same activity gave her so much distaste? Why was Pauline so often undressed, on her back or riding her stud, while Odette shrank from what she considered her wifely duties? It was something Odette hoped to find out some day, but just how she was unclear. Certainly her own husband had never given her the slightest sexual satisfaction. And she had not the will to take a lover herself, though most of the soldiers stationed at the plantation had given her smoldering glances from time to time. They understood full well the awful punishment that would befall them if they forced the second-in-command's wife into sexual congress, though with the General's own wife it appeared she was a law unto herself.

The siege of Crete-a-Pierrot was the last campaign of the war to win back the island of San Domingue for France. Though Dessalines, the rebel who held the stronghold, fought fiercely, the French forces finally managed to wrest it from him. Leclerc ordered three of his generals to attack the fortress from three points, weakening the position of Dessalines. At last his campaign succeeded and he conquered this last bastion of the rebel slaves, winning it after a long siege. Inside he found the outrageous atrocities that had been committed, with over 10,000 citizens, men, women and children with their throats cut. He also found almost that number left in the woods, whose lives would also have been forfeit had not Leclerc taken the position when he did.

Upon the surrender, he took all the black soldiers and officers into the French army, conferring on them the same positions they had held under the rebels and the insurrection collapsed, at least for the time being. There was no reason to believe that these same black troops would not rise up in rebellion once again, given the chance. For the moment, however, in March of 1802 it seemed the island was back in French hands.

Leclerc was at Port au Prince after his great victory, and sent for his wife and child, plus their attendants to join him. Pouting over the uncomfortable journey she would face, Pauline delayed as long as she dared, organizing her wardrobe and sending delaying notes via messenger over the mountains to the secure port in the two major westerly arms of the country. Finally, they took to the sea in a French Man-o-War and made the journey, guarded as ever by the faithful Duval and his troops, and arrived, hot and exhausted in Port au Prince. The family settled, at least temporarily, into the former Presidential Palace of L'Ouverture, and husbands and wives had time to catch up on the weeks when the men had been away, saving Saint Domingue for Napoleon and France. Pauline reported to Leclerc on Dermide's progress in counting and beginning to learn his letters, both of which had been accomplished by the governess, Mme. duBois, and none of it under his mother's supervision. She had been far too involved in her own pursuits – mainly long and hot sessions with Zeus – to pay much attention to the child, but she glossed over this fact when speaking with her husband. It was enough that she was now the toast of Port au Prince, all the troops singing her praises for her beauty, her wit and her intrepid interest in them. Occasionally she would ask about a wife or sweetheart back home, praising the particular soldier for his service to his country, smiling sweetly and offering her hand to kiss. This was enough for each individual so favored with her attention to spread the word of the delights of Mme Leclerc. She also was charming and gracious to the planters from the surrounding plantations who flocked to her entertainments: dinners, balls, musical evenings, raising her level of popularity to even greater heights. She seemed to eschew her former liaison with the giant slave, focusing all her sexual energy on her husband, who was more than happy to keep her content in this department.

Pauline seemed to shake off her tiredness quickly, as the entire garrison turned out to make her welcome. She enjoyed playing her part of the victor's wife to perfection. She banished Zeus, who had accompanied the party from La Colline Verte, to the servants' quarters – at least temporarily - and prepared to entertain her husband in the drawing room, the ballroom and, especially, the bedroom.

She ordered a milk and water bath in the bedchamber and bid Odette to attend her while she received her husband back into her life. Naturally, Odette would have preferred not to be present at the reunion of husband and wife, but she had no choice. At least it put off, if only for a little while, the confrontation with her own husband, who paced their bedchamber, waiting for his wife to join them there.

Pauline lounging in her tub, was in one of her most willful moods. She laid the bath sponge on her most private parts with such abandon as to cause Odette, who stood ready by her mistress, to help in her ablutions, to turn away in modesty. Surely, with Leclerc sitting in a long chair at the feet of his wife, did not want a third party to be privy to such intimacy between herself and the General? Pauline, however, had no such scruples. She alternately laved and stroked her breasts, the black hair between her legs and the labia and clitoris beneath it, sensuously and thoroughly. Leclerc's breathing became sonorous and he began to perspire in the air stirred up by the overhead fan, propelled by a small boy who rhythmically pulled a long string in the corner of the room. Odette knew that, when the actual coupling began, this boy would still be there, manning the fan. Like so many of her class, servants were all but invisible to Pauline. It would not have occurred to her to dismiss anyone of that status during any private moments – with her husband, or any other man. Such inferior beings should not be possessed either of eyes to see or a tongue to tell.

"I am ready," announced Pauline, putting down the sponge and preparing to rise from the murky waters. She held out her hand, which Odette grasped firmly, pulling Pauline's slight body from the water and standing her on a mat laid over the floor. She enveloped her mistress's body in a huge linen towel, and began to pat her dry.

Leclerc rose from his chair. "Let me do that, Madame." He supplanted Odette and took over the drying, leaving Odette to stand, helplessly before the couple. She could not withdraw until she was dismissed and neither Pauline nor Leclerc seemed, for the moment, to be aware of her presence.

She averted her eyes as best she could, without actually turning her back on the husband and wife who had begun to nuzzle each other and utter soft moans of pleasure.

Laughing, Pauline unbuttoned the front of her husband's trousers, letting them drop over his knees, She thrust her hand into one leg band, kneading and pulling the already burgeoning penis in her practiced grip. Leclerc moans became louder and he leaned down to take one of Pauline's rouged nipples between his lips, sucking loudly in pleasure.

She arched her back, her eyes raking the room. It was then she noticed her lady in waiting, still standing there. "You may go," she commanded, with a jerk of her head toward the open door.

Odette dropped a small curtsey and backed off, shutting the door behind her as she went. Behind her, the boy still pulled on his string, the better to fan his master and mistress as they made violent love to each other, totally oblivious of his presence in the corner of the room.

In her bedchamber, her own husband was awaiting her, already clad in his nightshirt. He sat on the edge of the bed, hem of the garment folded up above his waist, a stiff prick swinging before him.

"Come here, wife," he commanded. "I have been awaiting you this half hour while Monsieur and Madame frolic next door."

"Alas, not tonight," said Odette

"What? You disobey your husband?" His hand went up to strike her, but she caught it as it descended.

"It is the time of my monthly flux," she said, modestly lowering her eyes. Boucher, ever fastidious, would usually not even share a bed with her when she was in this condition. Odette prayed he would not discover her lie, for she had bled only the previous week. She had on her side a history of irregular fluxes, so if she was not in a similar condition at this time next month – should he still be around – she could plead that irregularity as an excuse not to have sex.

"Quel dommage!" he exclaimed. "And I so ready for you. Well, come here anyway. I can make use of you in another way."

Not knowing what was coming, she obediently drew closer to the bed.

"Kneel down," he commanded.

She obeyed.

"Open your mouth."

Wordlessly she did as she was told.

"Now, draw your lips over your teeth."

Pauline began to see what was coming but was helpless to gainsay this, her lord and master. She bowed her head and, again, did as she was told.

Leclerc guided his erection into her unwilling mouth. "Clasp your lips around me," he ordered. "Make sure your teeth do not graze me in any way. Keep them that way." He took his foreskin between his thumb and forefinger, forced it back and commenced to push himself in and out of her mouth. The first such thrust caused Pauline to gag, but a hard slap to the back of her head caused such pain she forced herself to concentrate, hoping it would soon be over. Fortunately, with the foreskin stretched as far back as he could hold it, Boucher experienced acceleration in his own pleasure, and with very few strokes he shot forth his load into his wife's unwilling mouth. She gagged again, willing herself not to vomit with the disgust of receiving such an unwanted gift. As soon as he withdrew she leaped to her feet, rushed over to the slop jar and spit out as much of the sticky, filthy stuff as she could. Behind her came her husband's furious voice.

"So you think so little of the elixir that causes children that you would void yourself of it. Come back here, Odette."

With no way out, she obeyed.

"I am going to punish you so you do not again so forget your place. And I will teach you to perform this act with better grace and more skill. Merde! The lowliest of prostitutes is more experienced than you." He grabbed her wrists, twisting them together and forcing her across his knees. Easily he lifted her skirts, throwing them over her head, and pulled down her loose knickers. His open hand descended on her naked buttocks, rhythmically and with deadly accuracy. The first slap caused Odette's breath to draw in, so painful was the blow. With subsequent ones, however, she began to experience a strange sensation, somewhere between pain and pleasure. A tingle started between her legs, which mounted and mounted to a frenzied feeling, engulfing her and causing her to rise upward on waves of sensation. With the tenth blow it was as if a huge bunch of fireworks exploded inside her, causing her to scream out with an animal sound that was totally unfamiliar to her ears, as she experienced her first violent orgasm. Certainly this petit mort, so gloried by others of her sex, was surely worth the pain inflicted by the man who was supposed to cherish her. She lay beside her snoring husband but a few moments later, red heat and pain radiating from her backside, joy and fulfillment within her womb.

For a few weeks the two couples remained at Port au Prince. Leclerc had noticed, while on various maneuvers around the island, the incredibly lush flora and fauna, consisting of many kinds of animals and plants that were unknown in France. It was his wish to export as many of these as possible, as gifts for his brother-in-law, thus reminding him of the incredible sacrifice that he, Pauline and Dermide had made to come to this far away island to save it for France. He and his wife also began their own zoo, and arranged for many of the exotic flowers to be planted back in Le Cap and at the plantation belonging to Odette. He researched newer and better ways to cut and process the incredibly rich fields of cane, for the export of this particular commodity would mean much revenue for France. With the island population no longer predominantly slaves, it was necessary to pay the workers who cut the cane and turned it into molasses as well as that much more valuable product: refined white sugar. The balance of paid labor versus the former slave labor was a major concern, and much time was spent in estimating the possible profits of the various plantations and how much of that would fall to the coffers of the Emperor. There were in place laws that stated the planters could only sell their cane and other commodities to France, at tariffs fixed by the central government in Paris. Such tariffs were most certainly not in favor of the planters, and there had long been smuggling of goods off the island, both by boat and through the rather porous border with the neighboring eastern end of the island, which was still under Spanish dominance. And, all along, it was necessary to deal with the gradients of color on the island: from the rich white plantation owners, through the poorer white merchants in the towns, through the mulatto population up to and including the blackest of the former slaves, ruled until Leclerc's astonishing victories by the formidable leader, Toussaint L'Ouverture. At the surrender of his generals to Leclerc, L'Ouverture had retired to his plantation on the northern shore of the island, there to be left in peace – he hoped and expected – for his lifetime. He did not take part in the general amnesty given to his officers. He vacated the Presidential Palace in Port au Prince, which was shortly taken over by Leclerc as his headquarters in that town. Unfortunately, Leclerc had other plans for this once powerful leader, plans which would be put into play somewhere further down the road.

For the time being, however, he was playing the part of husband and father, and writing many letters to his brother in law in France trumpeting his victories in Saint Domingue. From France came letters of commendation, and drawings of the latest French fashions, which thrilled Pauline, loving nothing better than to spend money on clothes. She summoned the best seamstresses the island had to offer and set them to work creating a whole new wardrobe as befitted the First Lady of the island. All this kept her from fretting over her separation from Zeus, who still waited on table and kept his eyes studiously away from the curves and white skin that had so delighted him back at La Colline Verte. Pauline, too, paid no attention to the massive black servant; to other eyes he was just another footman in the Leclerc household, unimportant and pretty much invisible.

Odette, too, replenished her wardrobe, though not with the total lack of abandon showed by her mistress. Nothing was too good for Pauline, no cost needed to be considered. With a much slimmer purse, Odette had to pick and choose carefully, even to the extent of making over some of the dresses she had brought out from France only months before. But it gave the women a purpose to their days, stuck as they were in this hot and humid climate which bred so many terrifying tropical diseases which decimated the white population of the island, especially the newly arrived French contingent. The Leclerc family, together with Odette and Boucher had, so far, avoided contracting the dreaded Yellow Fever, called then the Siamese Fever, which was had so thinned the ranks of Leclerc's army. Indeed, by the time he had subdued the island, the General was writing to France for much needed reinforcements. If dysentery, Dengue fever and other tropical diseases had not downed a large percentage of his soldiers, then the Yellow Fever was bound to get many of them – and did.

All was not gloom and doom, however, in the General's living quarters. A multitude of servants, plying their fans – both those suspended in the high ceilings and on long poles to waft cooling breezes above their masters and mistresses - served to make the days tolerable at least. And at night a breeze usually came up from the sea, cooling at least temporarily the habitations on shore. There were verandas to lounge on, and Pauline certainly took advantage of this aspect of island living. There were magnificent tropical flowers in the gardens, to which Leclerc devoted a few hours each day, directing the gardeners and laying out ever more elaborate schemes for them to execute. There were tropical drinks of citrus fruits and mangoes, sweetened with an unlimited supply of the product gleaned from the cane. There were entertainments as well, usually given in the relative cool of evening. Everyone who was anyone in the town was invited, and all donned their most resplendent garments to wait upon the Governor General and his Lady, though in the crowded rooms everyone perspired greatly, in spite of all the fanning. And sanitary arrangements were of the most primitive. The men availed themselves of the gardens, urinating all over the carefully laid out plants, while the ladies repaired to a small chamber off the front hall, to squat perilously over porcelain chamber pots, which were emptied frequently by the lowly servants assigned to this task.

And, as always, there was sex. Pauline's appetites still knew no bounds, and often she and Leclerc disappeared from the verandas for a whole morning or afternoon, repairing to their upstairs chamber where sounds of their lovemaking floated out the open French doors over the upstairs gallery and down to the first floor veranda. Indeed, some of the soldiers stationed around the house as guards spent their off hours speculating just what their general and his lady were up to up there above their heads. The cries and moans and squeals were almost continuous, and went on for many hours. Surely their leader was a man among men, a stud of the first water. For otherwise how could he possibly get it up countless times in a few hours? And counted the soldiers did, noting each screaming orgasm on the part of Pauline, leading to a brief period of silence before the moans commenced again.

Downstairs on the veranda, Odette would continue her sewing or reading, trying to pretend she heard nothing, waiting with distaste for the summons from her own husband to follow him upstairs and indulge him as well. She had learned that pleading her monthly courses did not work as a respite from sex; Boucher had proved that with the fellatio he had commanded and the hard spanking she had endured as a result of spitting out a mouthful of his sperm. She had resigned herself to his often brutal and totally without feeling sexual intercourse, closing her eyes and trying to think of something else while he either pumped away over her or thrust himself forcefully into her unwilling mouth. She knew now better than to spit out his semen, but swallowed it with as little gagging as possible. This was part of the bargain which was marriage, to be resigned to. Odette often wondered if Pauline was a rare exception to the belief that women did not enjoy the act of congress or if she herself was the odd one out. She had no other women with whom to compare the act of lovemaking; her only information came from her mistress, who was happy to discuss the sexual performance for endless hours.

One particularly hot afternoon in April, when the tropical sun was beating down with more strength than usual, both couples were upstairs in their respective bedrooms. In the corner of each room a small black boy plied his string to rotate the large fan overhead, supposedly oblivious to what was going on just feet away from his nose.

Odette was en negligee, sitting on the edge of the bed and awaiting her husband's pleasure. He was being particularly unpleasant today, ordering her about and not waiting more than a few seconds for her to comply with his instructions. She had been slow ordering a lemonade for him downstairs on the veranda, and had seemed reluctant to precede him up the stairs when he had insisted they repair to their bedroom. Both, in his opinion, were infractions of the wifely code of conduct he expected at all times, and both were deserving of punishment. His weeks in the fields, consorting with all manner of camp followers which always accompanied the army on maneuvers, had taught him some of the baser ways of satisfying himself, and he seemed to take delight in trying them out on his more refined and delicate wife. The more he managed to humiliate her, the more it aroused him, making his orgasms more intense and more satisfying than ever. And, with a long and otherwise boring afternoon ahead of him, he intended to indulge himself thoroughly.

He looked over at his wife, sitting on the bed, peignoir clutched modestly to her small breasts.

"Disrobe," he ordered brusquely

When she did not instantly obey, he strode over to her, crossing the floor in two large steps, and jerked the thin material, embellished with lace and ruffles, off her shoulders and over her arms. He had his riding crop in has hand, and gave her one short stroke across her smooth white thigh, raising a satisfactory welt.

Odette bit her lip against the pain, but made no other sound. She had learned that any indication of pain usually caused more pain.

"Lie down," Boucher then ordered.

This time Odette complied with speed. Perhaps he would enter her, thrust around a few times and ejaculate and that would be enough for him.

Roughly Boucher pushed apart her thighs, leaving his wife spread-eagled on the bed below him. He took the shaft of the riding crop, laying it over the black muff before him, and thrust it deeply into the tender labia, parting the lips of her sex and rubbing hard over the clitoris. There was no tenderness in the gesture, no thought that this might be pleasurable to her. It was solely for his lust, his necessity to dominate her and watching his wife squirm with pain on the bed beneath him seemed to rouse some primal instinct in him. He began to pant, moaning first softly then loudly, eyes boring into her face to see her reaction.

Instinctively, Odette closed her eyes, hoping to blot out the bestial desire she saw in her husband's own eyes.

Boucher dropped the crop and fell heavily onto the slender body. His erection sprung mightily from his own forest of black hairs, and he guided it with one hand into his wife's vagina, parrying and thrusting immediately into her dry insides. Even he realized this would not make the situation more pleasurable for him, and withdrew quickly, causing a wave of pain to sweep Odette. Somehow she managed to stifle any noise.

"Clearly you are unready to receive your husband," he said in an icy tone. "Open your mouth."

Squeezing her eyes more tightly shut, Odette complied. Her husband manipulated himself onto his knees, one each side of her head. His swinging meat, almost purple in color, swung over her, while his balls hung down over her chin, soft and somehow reminiscent of the ripe figs down in the garden. Almost she thought she would vomit, but at least her mouth was filled with saliva. She took him into the red cavern, remembering to fold her lips over her teeth as he had taught her and did not even retch when he almost rammed himself down her throat. He gave only a few short thrusts, then returned his attention to her nether regions, and once again rammed himself home into her quavering vagina. It was little more lubricated with the saliva she had spread over his hard on, but, for him, it was enough. He pumped hard, his body covering hers completely. He was so heavy she almost passed out from lack of oxygen, but at least he managed to achieve orgasm almost instantly, shouting out as he did so. He pulled out quickly, once again causing the searing pain, and collapsed beside her on the bed, now sticky with cum and hot perspiration from their exertions. Odette lay back miserably and prayed it was all over, at least for the time being. She was not to have her desire.

Boucher lay like a log for only a few moments, then felt for his flaccid penis and began to manipulate it, stroking and rubbing, giving short jerks, until the organ once again sprang to attention.

"Kneel up on the bed," he ordered.

Wondering what would happen next, Odette hastened to comply. The last time a spanking with his bare hand, this time it might well be the crop. She awaited her fate.

Boucher knelt before her, the stiff organ swinging between them. He thrust himself forward, pushing her breasts together and pushing his erection up between them.

"Take your hand," he ordered. "Stroke my testicles. Gently. Very gently. If you hurt me you will be punished."

As softly as she could, Odette reached down and cupped the swinging little sacs in her hand. They were hairy and slightly wrinkled, resting as they did in the loose skin of the scrotum. As softly as she could she stroked them, hoping not to anger Boucher who rubbed his penis up and down on her chest, between the globes of her breasts, held tightly together by his sweaty hands.

"Now, isn't this delightful," Boucher almost purred. "Doesn't this make you happy?"

Odette could only make a noncommittal murmur which might have meant anything, but Boucher chose to take it in the affirmative.

"You are such a cold bitch," he commented. "Not like those little trollops we have for our pleasure out in the field. "But you are young yet and you may still learn some of the tricks that satisfy a man."

His comments turned to groans, which turned to louder noises almost resembling singing, as Boucher came closer and closer to orgasm.

He threw back his head, emitting an animal wail, and sperm jutted up from between her breasts and covered her face in its stickiness. Boucher sank down onto the bed, leaving Odette kneeling above him.

"I hear it's wonderful for the complexion," he smirked. "Aren't you lucky?"

Odette could only stare down at him in silence, which, thankfully, he took for agreement.

"Shall we have another round?" he inquired. "First, though, a piss." He rose from the bed, pulled the china bowl from under his side, and aimed a rapid stream of urine at it. Missing slightly, some of the urine sprayed over the rim of the chamber pot onto the floor. Boucher gestured toward the black boy, still plying his string in the corner. "You, boy, clean this up. Now."

The boy leaped to his feet and padded down the corridor, returning momentarily with a wet rag with which he proceeded to clean up the urine. He took the rag and the chamber pot out into the hall, and returned to resume his endless pull on the string that operated the fan above the Bouchers' bed.

He lay back down on the wide mattress, turned away from Odette and fell into a light slumber. Soon he was snoring and Odette lay down beside him though as far away from her husband as possible. Through the next hour or two, while Boucher snored beside her, Odette started at the ceiling.

The next morning, the two generals were conferring in Leclerc's study, and Odette found time to make a request of her mistress.

Embarrassed, red faced, she half turned away from the other woman.

"Madame, may I ask you a question about...about...."

"Yes?" Pauline was ever ready to discuss the sexual act, happy to offer any suggestions another woman might want. "Do you wish to ask about the consummation of marriage between a man and a woman?"

"Yes." Odette's eyes were cast down, focused on a crack between two planks on the verandah floor.

"Do ask. Do not be shy. There are many a trick to making a man pleasure you."

"Uh. Well, about dryness. I mean, sometimes I do not seem to be ready...."

Odette immediately understood. "Of course, I understand. If a man has not successfully titillated you into such a flood of desire as to make it hard for him to enter you, then of course you must have help."

"Titillate?" Odette was unsure just what the word meant.

"Of course. Ready you for his entry into you. If you are not ready then it is not pleasurable for you. Indeed it can be quite painful. Though it is a feeling I never experience myself. Just to be near a handsome man, one with a bulge in his trousers is enough to cause my juices to flow and flow strongly. And when he strokes me there – ah – with his finger, with his thumb on my clitoris, or with his thing brushing the tender parts of my body, or his tongue between my legs..." Pauline paused, breath coming harder now, indeed, she was almost panting.

Odette looked miserable.

"Sometimes," Pauline continued gently, "when a man is mostly on the field of battle, he has no such niceties when he comes home to his wife. Then it must be she who takes the lead, lets him know what she likes, what makes her thrill to her touch."

Odette looked even more miserable.

Pauline finished quickly. All this talk of sex had so roused her she needed the act now, immediately. "And, if none of this works, there is always the salve I have obtained from one of the voodoo priestesses in the town. You just rub a little of it on the parts I have just mentioned and not only do you obtain the moisture you require, it seems to intensify your experiencing le petit mort. I will send a jar to your chamber when next I go upstairs. Which, come to think of it, is now. I am somewhat fatigued. Help me up."

Odette rose to obey.

"Oh, and please send a message to my husband that I wish him to join me. I have things to discuss. When he is finished with Boucher of course." She strolled into the hall and up the staircase. A few minutes later Pauline heard the heavier tread of Leclerc on the stairs. Apparently he had received the message and was joining his wife. Almost immediately the sounds of their lust wafted down to the veranda. So much for the things Pauline had wished to discuss. As always, she was true to form.

These idyllic days for the Leclercs, and miserable ones for Pauline, ended only short weeks later, when the General sailed for Le Cap in order to rebuild the town, leaving Pauline and her attendants behind. The general's lady chafed not at all at the absence of her husband, but once again installed the giant Zeus outside her door to the upstairs gallery, with the convenience his position offered to the delights of her bedchamber beyond the glass doors. The same noise of delighted sex emanated from the upstairs room, with the only difference that it was now Zeus who was romping there with Pauline, not her own husband. As usual, her pleasures came before anything else in Pauline's life.

Odette, however, was delighted with the departure of her husband with Leclerc. At least she was spared the daily and nightly sex forced on her by Boucher. Even with the small pot of salve that Pauline had contributed to her lady in waiting, sex continued painful – and humiliating.

At Le Cap, burned to the ground but two short months earlier, reconstruction had already begun and the roofs of the town were rising above the azure bay. The architect, who had traveled out with the expedition, was a man named Norvins, whose vision for the new French capital was nothing short of classical, modeled after the ancient structures of Greece and Rome. The new town was expected to be finished in short order, at which point Pauline could once again rejoin her husband and reign as the queen of this little colony so far away from France.

Leclerc wished that this expedition to the Antilles' would forever solidify his position with his brother-in-lay, earning him a much more important position when he returned to France. He hoped his exploits on Saint Domingue would raise him almost to the status of the First Consul, with his discovery of medicinal plants, exotic animals and even, the ownership of a property on the island. He desired the transfer of a small island to Pauline and him, which was a major producer of hard wood which would produce a princely sum for the couple as an annual income. He also wrote to Napoleon that he needed a further 12,000 troops, the original forces with which had sailed only months ago had been greatly depleted by tropical diseases. He also needed medical supplies and – always – more money with which to pay the troops he had and to rebuild. Since letters took at least six weeks each way to France, with the additional delay of a vote by the government granting his requests, he could not expect to hear back earlier than four or five months hence, which hampered his efforts on the island.

By early May enough of the town had been rebuilt for Pauline to again join her husband in Le Cap. The cooler situation of Odette's plantation above the town would be used for respite from the heat of the town, as well as the fear of contacting the deadly fever so prevalent at this time of year. From his exile L'Ouverture predicted that, with the advent of hotter weather, the yearly outbreak of the Siamese Fever would again be unleashed and the French troops would be further decimated.

Pauline inspired such adoration among the blacks on the island, that it was difficult not to find hoards of them following her about all during the day and far into the night. Many even wished to go indoors whenever Pauline did, making discipline and safety difficult for the soldiers who guarded the Governor General and his First Lady.

Leclerc finally devised a solution to this seemingly impossible situation: a huge party for these worshippers of Mme. Leclerc, all of whom were invited for a gala event some distance from the property in an open forest glade. There would be much food and native dancing for all to enjoy.

The extravaganza opened tamely enough, with scores of blacks descending on the glade, where Pauline was enthroned under an arbor the better to watch the festivities. Swinging over her head were sprays of wild roses and frangipani, scenting the air around her with their perfume. Odette sat at a little distance, and Dermide leaned against his mother's knee for all to behold and honor.

Soon, however, the sedate gathering turned into a bacchanal. Native instruments set up their lurid chorus, to be joined by the timpani of tom toms then the high percussion of voodoo drums, as the men and women began to whirl and writhe in abandon to the wild music. Louder and faster they jumped and swayed, losing all contact with reality as the frantic rhythm beat into their very veins. Hastily Pauline and her attendants withdrew back to the plantation house, while the natives continued their celebration, which by now had turned into an orgy, until dawn broke the next day.

Early June, when the heat had become ever more stultifying, brought a grim problem to the fore. Though Leclerc had guaranteed safety to L'Ouverture for his lifetime, with peaceful residence on his estate, now it was deemed necessary to arrest the former leader and transport him to France. It was necessary to break his word.

And so, acting on Leclerc's orders, General Bruner, one of the senior members of the Governor General's staff, was ordered to set up a meeting with L'Ouverture, ostensibly to discuss military matters concerning the island.

With no suspicion of what was going to happen, L'Ouverture met with General Bruner at the town of Les Gonaves, where he was summarily arrested and held for transport to France. He shortly thereafter was loaded on a military ship, together with his wife and two sons. He said, before departure, that never would the white man stop the forward march of history for his native San Domingue, even though he himself would not be there to see this day of total freedom come. In France he was imprisoned in a fortress in Jura, away from his wife and children who were left at liberty. It was here he died in just under a year, but the revolution which he had so helped to shape would continue on after his death.

Back in Saint Domingue, L'Ouverture's prediction of the Siamese Fever decimating the French troops was coming true, as the pestilence descended in June, wiping out many of the soldiers, and their officers, who had arrived on the island but a few short months before. The patients who entered the hospitals, bitten by the mosquitoes that carried the plague, usually died within twenty four hours. The fever was accompanied by vomiting, paralysis of the nervous system and final delirium, which led to death.

In spite of the huge numbers of his troops that were being lost, Leclerc was complacent in that he had put down the rebellion and restored order. Apparently Napoleon agreed with his brother in law. He wrote that he was planning tremendous rewards for Leclerc and his officers on their return to France, commensurate with the great loyalty and bravery they had exhibited on the field of battle in this far flung part of the Republic.

Leclerc was delighted with the news, which he immediately shared with his wife, followed by an especially frantic session of lovemaking, after which they dressed and organized a celebration party for all the aristocracy of the town swelled by the senior officers in the army. It showed Pauline at her best: gracious hostess, loving wife, sister to the First Consul of France.

Leclerc hoped to return to France in triumph the following spring, reputation bolstered to high acclaim by his exploits, riches and rewards to be heaped on his head once he regained his native soil. In the meantime, there was the social life of the town, now rebuilt, to enjoy and relaxing weeks in the hills above at La Colline Verte. All looked to be shining bright in those early summer weeks of 1803.

Chapter Five

Odette's Majority

Odette was happy to be back on more familiar territory, and was never happier than the days Pauline announced that they would all be repairing to La Colline Verte for periods from a long weekend to several weeks in residence there.

She enjoyed spending time with Jacques, who was the only link to her now dead parents. He told her of other years, before she was born, when her father first came to the island and fell in love with her mother, the daughter of a rich planter whose plantation above the town of Le Cap was called La Colline Verte. In a few short months they had married and, on the death of her grandparents, had inherited the plantation. Many white women withered and died in this tropical climate, from childbirth to the dreaded Siamese fever, but her mother had proved an exception, hale and hearty for a number of years and interested in everything from the running of the plantation and the production of cane, to the unusual ingredients the cook obtained to cook her famous gumbos and stews, so dear to the Creole heart and palate. Sadly, after many childless years, she had finally conceived, and borne a daughter who was Odette, her only child. During her time as chatelaine at La Colline Verte, one of her great pleasures was the garden, which she tended with the help of Jacques and a small army of under-gardeners.

The gardens, now redesigned by Leclerc, in the more formal fashion exhibited at Versailles, bloomed brilliantly in the tropical climate of much sun and even more rain, and Odette picked huge bouquets of fragrant tropical flowers which she arranged in vases for every room in the house.

Even Pauline seemed to enjoy these periods of relative tranquility, when she was free from the demands of entertaining and attending the theater, dinners and balls in other aristocrats' houses. She lounged around the verandah most of the day in the skimpiest and most diaphanous of costumes, only changing them for the more formal meals she took with her husband, Odette, Boucher and – sometimes – other staff members, including the ever attentive Duval. She sent supplies meant to comfort the sick troops, most suffering from Siamese Fever during the hottest months of June, July and August: custards and fruit drinks, light as air beignets turned out by the cook and her assistants in huge numbers, together with small bouquets from the abundance of flowers in the gardens, the better to cheer up the long wards overfilled so many soldiers some were forced to sleep on pallets on the floor. Her designation as a charmer and a lady bountiful did not diminish in that summer of 1803, and she basked in the adoration she felt all around her. Most of these activities were overseen, if not actually performed, by Odette, who expected no credit and none was forthcoming. If Pauline was happy, then Odette's life was easier, with her mistress making fewer demands on her time. This left her more leisure to expand her deepening relationship with Jacques – and to ride out more often with the ever-charming Colonel Duval. His ever polite interest in her and her concerns, not the least of which was the return of the plantation to its former level of sugar production, did much to assuage the mounting distaste with which she held her union with General Boucher. The sex, which had become more frequent, was simply a burden to be borne, and Odette had learned to think of other things – especially the brilliant blue eyes of Duval gazing sideways at her as they rode the acres of the plantation – and pray for the end of the supposed act of love.

Summer wore on, hot, humid and oppressive, a season to be borne. Everyone was looking forward to the slightly cooler days of autumn which should also bring a lessening in the number of cases of the Siamese Fever, which was so decimating the French troops. Indeed, of the 12,000 replacement soldiers requested by Leclerc some months before, only a quarter of that number had actually been sent out to Saint Domingue, and a full half of these immediately came down with the fever, with most dying of it. It would appear that L'Ouverture's prediction that he and his men need only hide out in the hills until summer, at which time this virulent plague would take care of the French invaders of the island. L'Ouverture himself by this time was already in France, where he would die within the year.

Remarkably, with the fever all around them, none of the Leclerc household became really ill. They had short bouts of the disease, with its attendant sweats, vomiting and high temperatures, but none developed into the more aggressive form of the illness, which killed so many people that long, hot summer on Saint Domingue.

Pauline usually emerged from one of these periods of illness more determined than ever to make life one long party, and would bid the officers and such wives as had made the trip with their husbands, along with the upper echelons of the population of the town, to her endless soirees, musical evenings and dinners. She had her own trained band of mulatto musicians to play at such events, and they made a splash of color among the pale court dresses of the women guests in their vivid uniforms. Though not Paris, not by a long shot, Pauline nonetheless lorded it over everyone else on the island by virtue of her position as wife of the Governor General. She consoled herself by realizing that, if she were back in the French capital, she would be taking a distinct second position to Napoleon's wife, Josephine, and even to her sister, Caroline, who was married to Murat who held the position of Commandant of Paris. The younger sister who had always been eclipsed by Pauline was now riding around Paris in a fashionable carriage, bedecked with jewels, playing second fiddle only to Josephine in the court that had sprung up around the First Consul. Pauline, as wife of a Colonial General, albeit he was also Governor General of Saint Domingue, would most certainly have found herself down the line of importance at her brother's court. Though Leclerc had considered sending her and Dermide back to Paris that summer, to ensure their safety, Pauline demanded one hundred thousand francs from her husband to make the trip. She was determined not to show up as the poor relation; she would need a carriage the equal – or the superior – to Caroline's, and sufficient jewels to take her proper place in the hierarchy of the Bonaparte family.

Leclerc was unable to provide these funds. He had been sending regular payments to his brother, in order to refurbish and expand his French property, Montgobert, adding a large conservatory, an aviary and zoo and additions to the house itself, more suitable, he felt, for the Victor of the Antilles and his Lady when they returned to France. Alas, this vision was never seen by him.

The Leclerc family moved frequently between the Governor General's residence in Le Cap, hastily rebuilt but functioning once again as the most sophisticated and fashionable town on the island, and Odette's plantation up in the hills, where it was marginally cooler, though not by much.

Of the two, Pauline enjoyed town living more. There was still a fairly large number of aristocrats who had lived on the island for several generations, swelled by the few wives who had come out with their husbands to Saint Domingue. Her mulatto orchestra practiced steadily the better to entertain Pauline's guests at her soirees, while the cooks in Pauline's kitchen experimented with new dishes to tempt the appetites of the party goers. At the plantation, the occasional neighbor rode over for luncheon or afternoon tea, but there was far less entertaining, which gave Pauline more time for her other favorite pastime: sex. She summoned her husband to her bedchamber at all hours of the day, and the nights were punctuated by her cries of lust as she and Leclerc practiced more and more exotic positions in stimulating themselves even more erotically. Pauline had picked up some pointers from watching the blacks' bacchanal, when the wild voodoo drums had caused such havoc and couples were copulating openly on the dance floor. She had also consulted a few of the wise women of the plantation, those who had encyclopedic knowledge of birth, death and all things sexual, and who had prepared certain potions and lotions to stimulate the sexual organs of both men and women, bringing them to ever more heightened orgasms. She shared some of these secrets with Odette, ever hoping that her waiting woman would come to enjoy the act of sex as much as she herself did.

One hot summer morning, the women were taking their coffee together on the upstairs loggia outside Pauline's rooms. The General's wife was glowing in the aftermath of a wild sexual romp with her husband, which had lasted most of the night and left her this morning limp, exhausted, but radiant. Her skin glowed and she almost seemed to be purring as she sipped her first cup of the hot, sweet liquid.

"Ah, Odette," she breathed. "Such joy as I experienced last night with Charles. I can hardly describe it." A sly smile spread over her beautiful face, one Odette knew meant a long litany of confidences she would rather not be privy to, but which she must hear with as much patience as she could muster.

"He began by blowing, ever so softly into my ear, which roused my senses beautifully, the covered my face with his kisses and my inner mouth with his tongue." Pauline smiled at her remembrance of her husband's ardor. "He then used his tongue to minister to my neck, and his lips to suck me. Tiens!" She indicated her throat where a large bruise was spreading over its smooth skin. "A love bite, see?"

Odette nodded.

"Such thrilling sensation was caused by this bite," she sighed. "I was ready to receive him then and there but no! He had other plans for me." She wiggled a little in her chaise, closing her eyes for a moment, leaning back into the pillows. She looked like a sleek cat which had just been at the cream.

82

"He continued down to my breasts, where he slowly stroked and sucked, raising my nipples to hard little nuts." Her hand caressed those breasts, which were now exposed between the lacy lapels of her morning peignoir, lazily and without shame.

Odette turned slightly away and pretended to watch a fat bee perched on the bougainvillea that overhung the loggia. Her lack of interest deterred Pauline not a whit.

"I thought I would climax but no, I managed to restrain myself as my beloved continued down, down, over my stomach, into my nether regions. He parted my lower hairs with a finger, and inserted his tongue between the lips of my outer sex, then found the seat of all pleasure and began to lick and such it with such finesse I actually climaxed then and there. My husband but chuckled, knowing I was capable of doing so many times during any session of lovemaking. I think my maximum was six within one time period. Can you climax more than once with your husband?" she inquired genially.

Odette was ready to squirm at the question, but her mistress had little interest in her answer and seemed satisfied with Odette's noncommittal murmur.

"Yes, of course. Where was I? Oh, yes, Charles had his tongue in play over my woman's parts and did not stop. I came down from one height and immediately started up again; this time it was like an explosion, a shooting off of a million cannons, a continuous fusillade. I actually think I passed out for a moment from sheer joy."

Odette found no need to comment; Pauline seemed to have become her own best audience.

"That, however, was not enough, for me or, especially for him. Remember, all this time he was the giver and I, the receiver. I know it was time for me to pleasure him." She gazed off for a moment into space.

"I indicated to him that he should lie on his back on the bed," she went on. "And I immediately mounted him, but not facing him, oh, no! I was going to give him the most intense pleasure a woman could give; I was going to perform the act of pompoir on him. Are you familiar with this position?"

Again Odette murmured a non-committal word and wished she could stop her ears against any further confidences from Pauline.

"I turned my back to his face and positioned my derriere on his stomach, then rose to take his manhood into my inner parts, using my hand at the base of his penis and tickling his testicles all the while. I have done many hours of exercises to strengthen my inner muscles and can now clamp and close them at will. It is said this is the position most favored of all by men in Araby, and women who can perform it are prized above all others. Well, I can perform it with the best, and did so for my beloved husband. All the while he was breathing so hard I thought I would kill him, and moaning so loud I thought he would wake the dead." Pauline let out a little giggle. "And when finally he achieved his climax, I could feel all that beautiful sperm shoot up inside me, which caused another such huge explosion also in me that again, I almost swooned."

She licked her lips hungrily and again sank back into the cushions. Her hand almost involuntarily reached down between her legs, bare now with the peignoir flowing back over the sides of the chaise. Pauline was, in fact, as naked as if she had been wearing nothing. Her fingers engaged in the softness between her legs, stroking and thrusting with abandon, oblivious to the other woman seated but a few inches away from her.

Suddenly she opened her eyes. "I need to use the chamber pot," she announced in a husky whisper. "Help me up."

Obligingly, Odette held out her hand and assisted her mistress to her feet. Pauline swayed across the boards of the porch and disappeared through the open French doors to her chamber, which she did not bother to close. From the loggia Odette heard the sounds of sexual pleasure as Pauline brought her self swiftly and efficiently, to orgasm. A moment later she called out to Pauline to attend her, and the lady in waiting rose and entered the bedchamber, where her mistress was lying spread eagled on the bed, her most private parts exposed to anyone entering the room. Pauline averted her head.

"I will rest for a while now," she announced. "But please send word to my husband that I wish to see him in an hour or so whenever he can spare the time."

Odette knew this was tantamount to a direct order, one which Leclerc rarely, if ever, ignored. She also knew that in the hour following, Pauline would once again be ravenously, extravagantly, engaged in more sex. For a woman who appeared to delicate that she was often carried from place to place by a giant black servant, whose sole job this was, she could certainly engage in a marathon of sex. Perhaps it was this which so exhausted her she could often not walk. Odette merely bowed her head to indicate she understood, and left the room to seek a servant to take the message to Leclerc that his presence was requested in his wife's bedchamber an hour hence.

Happy to escape - at least for the morning - her mistress's demands, Odette returned to her own chamber and donned her riding habit. She hoped Duval would be able to accompany her but if not there were plenty of officers deployed around the property who would be more than happy to accompany Mme. Boucher on her morning ride.

She was in luck for Duval was just crossing the verandah as Odette descended the steps to the first floor.

"Ah, Madame," the Colonel exclaimed, removing his hat from his head and sweeping her a low bow. "How enchanting you look. May I accompany you on your ride?

"It would be my pleasure if you would ride out with you," Odette murmured, dipping into a brief curtsey. Duval lifted her hand to his lips, brushing them across the knuckles, sending a brief thrill of delight upward from the secret place between Odette's legs, which up to now had never truly been engaged in the act of love. She wondered idly that, given a different man, a different situation from the distasteful sessions with her own husband if she, too, could not learn to enjoy the many pleasures Pauline was fond of recounting to her. But no, she pushed the thought away. Though Pauline took lovers by the dozen, apparently with the complete acceptance of her husband, she could never do such a thing. The bonds of matrimony, however distasteful, were sacred and not to be broken. She sighed and went out into the hot, humid morning.

The two horses were standing docily, held by a small black boy. Duval helped her onto the bay mare, lifting her easily into the saddle by her slender waist. His warm hands felt so good that Odette let out an involuntary sigh, either for the nearness of the handsome Colonel or the lack of attention she received from her own husband; she could not be sure which was the more accurate.

Duval easily swung himself into his own saddle, and the horses started side by side down the long driveway toward the distant fields of cane and the even more distant mountains. Even at the early hour, insects were sending up their humming cry and the sun burned fiercely in the sky of pale gold. It would be a scorching day, one guaranteed to sap the energy from all but the most hardy.

They skirted alongside the nearest field, peopled with sweating blacks who were engaged in hacking the cane down with their long machetes. The men swung the blades while the women lifted and stacked the heavy stalks onto waiting carts to transport them to the mill. Small children traversed the rows bearing gourds full of water with which to sustain the adult workers. Even a few minutes in such heat could fell the strongest of them and it behooved the overseers to make sure ample liquid was at hand. In the distance, smoke rose over the mill where the cane was being processed into molasses and that much more valuable commodity, refined white sugar. The plantation was not yet in full production, but it was slowly returning to its former quotas, traded for so many years for the goods and chattels sent out from France, which made the life of the rich planters tolerable and even luxurious.

"You have an excellent asset at hand, Madame," Duval said to Odette. "You must be very proud of this inheritance from your parents."

"My husband is counting every sou, believe me," Odette replied. "He is trying to figure out how to realize the highest possible production rate when we are no longer here. He is seeking the right overseer to wrest the most possible production from the cane once we have gone back to France."

"Do you think that is possible?" asked Duval.

"Nothing works so well as having the owners in residence," said Odette. "No overseer could possibly have the same interest in production. I fear once we leave this island things will fall back as they were while my parents were gone, and the income he hopes to realize will not materialize."

"And would you like to stay here, Madame, when the General and his family have sailed for France?"

Odette turned her eyes to gaze over the enormous fields of cane, stretching out before them in an unbroken vista which seemed to creep up to the very mountains. "I am not sure," she replied, so low that Duval had to swing sideways out of his saddle the better to hear her. "Somehow I feel I belong here, which is very odd considering we left Saint Domingue for France when I was barely out of the cradle."

"Yet the land is calling to you?"

"It is," said Odette slowly. "It is a strange sensation which I cannot understand."

"My own family holdings in France just got smaller and smaller with each successive generation," said Duval. "By the time I came along there was really nothing left of the land for me, which is why I joined the army."

"Would you wish for land, instead of a career as an officer for Napoleon?"

"Yes, I think so. Somehow my roots seem to lie in that direction. Not that I am adverse to serving our First Consul, laying down my life for France if necessary," he hastened to add.

"I hope it will not come to that, Monsieur. I would miss you." Cheeks aflame after this indiscreet admission, Odette touched her heel to her horse's side and cantered off ahead of Duval down a grassy track toward a patch of forest in the distance.

He gripped with his knees, and his own horse broke into a canter, following Odette closely along the track and into the relative shade of the wooded glade a half mile distant. They walked the horses, side by side again, deeper into the trees until they came to a mossy glade, overhung with the most brilliant orchids. Duval slid to the ground and held out his arms to help Odette dismount. She placed her hands on his shoulders and jumped to the ground. For a moment she was in his embrace, but freed herself and went to sit on a mound in the middle of the glade. Duval threw himself down beside her, craning his head back to look up at her face. For a moment neither of them spoke. Duval broke the silence,

"You must know how I feel about you...'" he began.

At the same time Odette said "We should not be alone together like this..."

"I only know I love you," Duval said, taking her hand again and bringing it to his lips, where he lingered, kissing between each knuckle, then turning it over to gently lick the palm with his hot tongue.

Odette gave a low moan and leaned up against the Colonel, thinking of nothing but his nearness and the masculine smell wafting from his body.

Duval clasped her in his arms, tipping her head up in order to kiss the sweet lips he had loved so long. At first it was a chaste meeting of their lips, but he very soon pressed harder then opened her mouth gently with his tongue in order to taste the sweet nectar within.

His ardor deepened, as Odette responded to his mouth and tongue, and he ran his hand over her lovely breasts, contained as they were in the tight jacket of her riding habit. He managed to unfasten the buttons, freeing her breasts into his probing hands, wringing a moan of pleasure from her. He bent to take those rosy nipples between his lips, sucking gently as they hardened beneath his tongue.

Odette was powerless before his advances, thrilling to his touch, which was sending signals of desire throughout her inner sex which radiated throughout her body. Was this was what she had been missing?

Were Pauline's stories about the wonder of sexual congress true? For a moment she seemed to float above the trees, observing a man and a woman in the throes of delight in the forest glade.

With a loud moan of his own, Duval reached down and flipped up the skirt of the habit, moving his hand to where the black springy hair of her bush met the inviting V at the top of her legs.

Odette suddenly came back to herself. She wrested herself away from the Colonel and managed to sit back up, pulling her jacket across her bare breasts as she did so.

"I am sorry, Colonel," she said, unable to look him in the face. "I hold myself true to the bonds of matrimony which I hold to be the sacred bond for men and women to indulge in these pleasures. I cannot have congress with you, I simply cannot." The last came out as a little sob.

Duval immediately straightened himself beside her, pulling away and folding the skirt once again over her legs. "Of course, Madame," he announced somewhat stiffly. "I quite understand. I forgot myself, so enamored of you have I become. It was inexcusable and have no fear, it will not happen again." He rose to his feet and stretched out his hand. "Please allow me to assist you to remount and we will continue your ride. I apologize if I have offended you." He stood there, silent, awaiting her commendation of his actions.

None came. Odette straightened her skirt and did up the buttons on her jacket, then held out her hand for him to help her to rise. "You have not offended me," she said evenly. "Indeed, you have honored me with your attentions. If I were not joined to Boucher, things might be different between us. But I am not like my mistress, I cannot consort with a man other than my husband, much as I might like to. I am glad you understand."

"I understand all too well. As I said, it will not happen again. Your proximity made me forget myself which transgression with not be repeated. Shall we mount and continue our ride?"

"Yes, let us do so," said Odette. She allowed the man to lift her again into her saddle, but this time his hands were not so warm on her body and they did not linger an instant longer than necessary. They took up their reins and once again rode along beside the vast stretch of cane fields that belonged to La Colline Verte.

That summer Leclerc doubled his efforts to collect more exotic flowers, plants, birds and animals to send back to France for the zoo in Paris. He also gave orders, through his brother, to implement the building of an aviary at his French estate, together with a greenhouse to hold the tropical plants he intended sending back, and two additional wings on the house, such renovations and additions to be undertaken with all due haste. He hoped to see the embellishment of his property in the following year when he and Pauline planned on returning to France. All as not going well with the truce he had established, however. The black generals, who had come over to his side as part of the armistice were making rumblings again about rebelling, in part due to the reprehensible treatment of the revered Toussaint L'Ouverture who had by now arrived in France and imprisonment in a cold and dreary cell near the mountains of Switzerland. All this took a toll on the general, who had recurrent bouts of fever which sapped his strength, together with the incessant sexual demands of his wife. Much as he enjoyed his vigorous romps with her, their frequency and length .took a further toll on his energy, leaving him unfit at times to attend to his many military duties.

Pauline, meanwhile, continued relatively healthy, exhibiting at no time the symptoms of the dreaded Siamese Fever. She even took her turn nursing soldiers in the military hospital, further inspiring adoration among the troops of her husband's army. She continued her soirees, though with limited guests as more and more people died of the dreaded Fever, and was ever ready with sexual pursuits whenever Leclerc was at home. When he was away – as he was frequently in the months following the armistice - she consoled herself in the arms of others. Sometimes it was the huge Zeus, who still slept before her door. Other times it was with a member of Leclerc's staff, or even some of the common soldiers guarding the Governor General's family. It was her habit to be carried to her bath, in the arms of the ever present Zeus, who performed this task dressed only in a loin cloth. As she luxuriated in her tub she would have paraded before her the choice of a bedmate for that day; no man who viewed Pauline in her bath ever refused and the stories circulated around the barracks became more and more lewd in nature as the sexual excesses of the General's Lady became general knowledge. That her husband seemed complicit in these liaisons was well known. No member of the military, whatever his rank, had the slightest fear of being disciplined for his servicing Pauline. On the other hand, her lady in waiting, Odette, had the reverse reputation. She was known as a lady of the highest moral character, one who would under no circumstances be untrue to her own husband. Knowing the cold rigidity with which Boucher always held himself, there were bets made about just how long Odette would put up with that icy reserve before she, too, capitulated and took a lover. So far the odds were with chastity, and many a soldier lost his bet on Leclerc's wife's fidelity.

Odette was often required to help at Madame's bath, along with her personal maid and the servant who carried her two and from her ablutions. It was an embarrassing time for the lady in waiting, who was repulsed by Pauline's free and easy ways with men. She often wondered why Leclerc put up with his wife's many infidelities, then welcomed her favors during the periods he was in the house. When he was away his back seemed totally turned to his wife's many indiscretions. It was a puzzle Odette never was able to solve.

One particularly hot morning, she had been summoned to the bathing chamber, which adjoined the bedchamber Pauline shared with her husband...when he was home. When he was not, there was a large variety of men coming and going at all hours, some black, some white. Pauline had attempted to discuss the relative merits of both colors with Odette, but had met with no success. Odette had slept with but one man, her husband, and had no other sexual experience at all, which still puzzled Pauline greatly.

Mme. Leclerc arrived borne in the arms of the gigantic black servant, Zeus, and lowered ever so gently into her concoction of milk and water, heated just to the tepid temperature she required. She sank back gracefully beneath the murky mixture, closing her eyes in pleasure.

Pauline remained in this position, then opened her eyes and summoned the first candidate to join her in the chamber. She motioned to the maid to begin washing her, and the woman picked up a large sea sponge and stepped into place beside the tub.

A young private stepped over the threshold, pausing, red faced in the doorway. He knew why he had been summoned and knew there was no way out of the situation. In any case, he had been assured by his comrades that he would be enjoying a morning of pure bliss, wrapped in the arms, and lying in the bed of the woman known universally as probably the greatest lay since Cleopatra. And having sex with Pauline would probably advance his career as well, since she managed to have promoted those in the army who especially pleased her.

Pauline raised one white hand and beckoned the young man to come closer to the tub. "Come here near me," she commanded. "I would see you better."

The man moved slowly toward the tub, his sword clanking against his high boots.

"Bring a stool," demanded Pauline.

The maid dropped the sponge and hastened to obey.

"Sit down beside me," cooed Pauline. "Do remove your sword; you have no need of it in here. Perhaps those hot boots as well."

Red faced, the man obeyed, then sank down on the stool placed within reach of Pauline's wet hand which now dangled over the side of her tub.

"My, what a handsome young man," she purred. "How old are you?"

"Eighteen, my lady," the man replied.

"And already serving my brother."

"To the death, Madame," the man replied proudly

"Well, you may come to the attention of my brother, depending...." She paused, but everyone in the room understood what she meant.

"Remove your tunic, soldier," commanded Pauline, 'and your socks."

The youth hastened to obey, dropping these garments to the floor and clad now only in his trousers.

Pauline stretched out the small white hand and stroked the man's groin through the thick fabric of the trousers. "I think we could do better than this," she remarked. "Undo those buttons." The trousers were buttoned each side and the man fumbled with the buttons, finally leaving the front flap at easy access to Pauline's roving hand. She thrust it down the front, causing the soldier to let out a gasp as her hand found its quarry. Expertly she gave a few swift strokes beneath the fabric, making the penis stand to attention, bulging the fabric over his groin to an almost unimaginable height. "I heard you were well-endowed," Pauline said. "Just what I like. You needn't show your member to the other ladies here. No doubt they would want you for themselves. However, for the morning at least you are mine. "Marie Claire," she ordered the maid, "my towel. Odette, order some wine to be brought to my chamber, along with some fruit. I may need to refresh myself later."

No one questioned what later meant.

Pauline gestured to Zeus. "Carry me back," she commanded. "And you," this to the soldier, "follow me." She allowed herself to be lifted and borne back through the door to her chamber. The young man, clutching his trousers as best he could over his hugely bulging erection, stood up and followed her.

Odette was happy to escape, find Jacques and relay the mistress's orders. The major domo was, as always, hovering in the hall, the better to be called to execute orders from anyone in the house who needed anything. He noticed the flushes aspect of Odette's face and suggested she might want to repair to the veranda, where he would fetch her a cool drink after carrying out Pauline's orders. Odette was only happy to comply. She sank down into a long chair and picked up one of the many palmetto fans placed around the house for just this purpose. She leaned back tiredly, waving the fan in front of her hot face. From upstairs came the unmistakable sounds of Pauline's session with the latest young man caught in her web.

In July of that summer of 1803 Leclerc wrote an enthusiastic letter to his brother in law in Paris, telling him that celebrations were planned in Saint Domingue, both for the return of the Island to French control and in honor of the French Republic's tenth anniversary. While celebrations would go on in Paris, Leclerc's plans for the island's fete never materialized. His military successes in May had brought only an uneasy peace, and the black troops and officers that had come over to his side were slipping away at a rapid rate. Plus which Leclerc's own troops were thinned out considerably with the tropical diseases contracted on the island, foremost of which was the dreaded Siamese Fever which felled men by the scores and in quick order. He and his family spent more and more time at the plantation up on the higher elevation behind Le Cap, both because it was marginally cooler than in town, and because the Fever had not spread this far, though the town and the ships an anchor were losing frightening numbers of souls daily.

Pauline, after doing her nursing stint while still at the Residence in Le Cap, and sending supplies to those in the hospital, seemed to forget the pestilence going on all around her once in residence at La Colline Verte. As long as she had her daily baths, a great deal of rest in the specially slung hammock sling on the verandah and plenty of sex, either with her husband when he was home, or with anyone else when he was not, she seemed content. In contrast to her mistress, as the long summer lingered Odette was becoming more and more restless. She had much time on her hands, since Pauline was so often 'resting' and did not require so much time from her lady in waiting, sewing, reading aloud or just plain gossiping. For the rest of her life Pauline would claim that the year spent in the tropics had vastly sapped her energy, and could only walk for very short distances and needed to be off her feet much of the time.

Odette was turning twenty-one that July, and Pauline was planning on a large celebration for her at the Residence in Saint Domingue. However, the Siamese Fever had taken such hold on both the town and the French fleet in the harbor that her plans had to be scrapped for a more modest party at the plantation. There would be only the Governor General's immediate family, Odette and Georges Boucher and some of the officers of Leclerc's staff, together with the gentry from the neighboring plantations, for the gala on July 17. Naturally Duval was among this number.

Though he and Odette still rode out many mornings, any possibility of intimacy had vanished after their encounter in the forest glade. He would not have betrayed her sense of loyalty in any way and she, however much she might have enjoyed his love – and his caresses – was unable to bring herself to cuckold her husband. It was a situation that was causing mounting tension in Odette, but she had no way of changing the situation. Boucher was her husband, she felt the need to obey him in all things, and his brand of lovemaking had not changed. She was trapped in a loveless marriage that stretched unceasingly into the future.

Pauline's enthusiasm for the upcoming birthday, however, at least made a diversion from the thoughts that whirled around in Odette's head most of the day and often long into the night. Her mistress was busy, when her energy allowed it, conferring with everyone on the plantation who would be involved in the gathering, from the chef and his assistants, to the seamstresses, to the vendors of the wines and other delicacies which would be sent up from Le Cap to the most important one of all: Jacques, who would be overseeing the whole. He seemed to be taking an inordinate amount of interest in the gala, organizing the small army of servants who would be waiting at dinner, to the menus and wines to the table settings, right down to the flowers which would be picked shortly before dinner commenced, the better to keep them fresh as long as possible.

Odette tried to discuss all this frantic activity with Boucher one night after they had retired. It was still stiflingly hot, and even the fan, pulled by the tireless black child in the corner of their bedchamber seemed to bring little relief.

"It is wonderful of Madame to go to so much trouble for my birthday," she remarked to her husband, as she sat brushing her hair out at her dressing table.

He lolled behind her on the bed partially undressed, idly scratching his penis through the fabric of his trousers.

If Odette hoped to divert his attention away from the inevitable sexual romp he was contemplating, she was disappointed.

"Yes, yes," he answered. "I hear all about it from the officers who expect to be invited. It seems they have nothing else to look forward to, now we have subdued those black bastards and sent L'Ouverture to prison in France. You would think nothing else is going on anywhere in the island, which is not true. There are still pockets of rebellion which must be put down. I have spoken to Leclerc on the matter, and he assures me all is well. I think he is wrong."

"But everyone is going to so much trouble," Odette protested gently. "Everyone here is thinking about the placement of the tables and the food and wine...and what the ladies' will wear."

Boucher snorted. "What fascinating topics. I have no interest in any of them. Now come here." He patted the bed beside him. "I feel somewhat jaded tonight. Time, I think, to teach you a few more tricks to pleasure and excite me."

Trembling, the party forgotten, Odette crossed the room as slowly as she dared to join her husband for whatever degradation he had in store for her. She did not want to be punished again as he had a few weeks before, even for the momentary pleasure it had given her. She wanted to experience the true glory and closeness of love, though knew it would never happen with this leering, red faced man splayed across their bed. She settled herself beside him, wishing the bed was wider so as to allow more space between them.

"Take off your garment," he ordered.

Odette untied the ribbons holding her peignoir around her waist and Boucher roughly pushed it off her shoulders, exposing her rounded breasts and the thicket of black hair far below them.

"Nice," he murmured unexpectedly, "oh, so nice." He grasped one breast, pulling and twisting it, causing Odette to cry out.

"Like it, my lovely?" grunted Boucher. "I thought so. You are finally beginning to appreciate the expertise of my lovemaking. He continued to pull and knead, while Odette clamped her lips tightly together, the better to let no more sound escape.

Mercifully, he finished his exploration of her breast, giving the nipple one final tweak, and turned his attentions downward. "Now how to enter that special cavern which you reserve only for me?" he mused to himself. "I know a new way."

Odette remained still.

"Turn over on your stomach," he commanded. "That's it. Now get up on your knees. Put your head in the pillow."

Wordlessly she obeyed.

"Thrust your derriere in the air. Higher, No, higher than that." He gave her a fierce slap on her buttocks, swift and painful.

Almost smothered in the pillow, Odette hastened to try for what he wished, and thrust her backside higher and higher. She seemed to satisfy Boucher, who positioned himself behind her, half kneeling himself. He took his prick, stiff and ready to enter her, into his hand and gave a couple of squeezes. "Might as well make the iron rod," he remarked to no one. "The better to thrust into that quavering hot cunt."

One more squeeze and he guided himself to the entrance of her vagina, parting the lips of her labia with his erection, then giving a sudden deep thrust, which drove him fully into her soft interior. With no preparation, Odette was dry and the rasp of her husband's penis on the tender interior of her vagina caused massive pain. Still, she managed to bite a corner of the pillow and remain silent. He usually finished faster when she did not participate in any way, and Odette hoped this would happen now.

Groaning loudly, clutching at her breasts from his position behind her, Boucher ground away, faster and faster, until he let out the loudest groan of all and collapsed, pinning him beneath her. Odette, inflamed from within, hardly breathing into the pillow, could but be grateful that once again, their sexual congress was over, at least for the time being. She prayed he was too tired, or had had enough to drink, not to want her again.

A few moments later Boucher rolled to his side of the bed, this time giving a different sort of groan, one of actual pain.

"Those damn crayfish at dinner. I swear, they have turned my insides to jelly." He rose quickly from the bed and crouched down on the chamber pot, so conveniently located underneath. An explosive bowel movement, combined with farts and odious air permeated the room, causing Odette to gag. She heard the liquid shit splat into the chamber pot, again and again and again. Almost she rose to fetch a scented handkerchief from her dressing table, but managed to remain inert.

At long last Boucher rose from his exertions and fell heavily across the bed. "Have the servant empty the pot and bring a clean one," he ordered.

Odette gave the necessary instructions to the servant at the fan rope, who rose immediately and performed the disgusting task. He was soon back with a fresh pot, which he placed in the space occupied by the former one, and went back to his string to pull the fan.

Boucher lay beside his wife, groaning. "I will have the cook whipped," he announced. "For serving such slop."

Odette did not point out that they had all eaten this same 'slop' and, so far, Boucher seemed to be the only one affected. He continued to complain for the next few minutes, then fell into a light slumber, in which he continued to groan much of the night, keeping Odette awake.

It was two days before her birthday party.

The next morning, he seemed to be somewhat recovered and rose at his usual time. Though pale and sweating slightly he managed to call his valet, dress and go downstairs for his morning conference with Leclerc, which they did over breakfast on the veranda. The ladies breakfasted in their rooms, off trays brought by house servants, and did not appear downstairs until later in the morning.

Arrangements for the party took over for the next couple of days, with servants running here and there and crates and barrels of supplies being delivered from the town to the kitchen shed for many hours. Though Boucher would have liked to have the cook flogged, it was not possible, for such a punishment would have made him unable to perform his magic over the food planned for Odette's feast.

During these two days Jacques was rushed off his feet, but each time he passed Odette, on the porch, in the hall, waiting at table, his eyes seemed to bore into her with an intensity she did not understand. She put it down to tension over the party, and thought no more of it. On the afternoon of the party itself, however, he came to her while she was resting in the hammock, usually occupied by Pauline, which was slung in the shadiest corner of the verandah. Pauline and Leclerc were upstairs in their chamber, and the unmistakable sounds of their lovemaking floated down to the lower floor. Everyone had pretty much learned to ignore these sounds, so frequent were they.

"Madame," he began, bowing before her. "May I speak with you a moment?"

"Of course, Jacques," answered Odette. "What is it? Some crisis in the kitchen? Did cook over spice the crayfish bisque?"

"No, Madame, nothing like that." Jacques seemed uncertain how to continue.

"Please go on,"

"You may recall I told you how many years I had been servant in this house, first to your mother and father, then, after her death, to your father and you until he sailed with you for France. You were but a small child and no doubt do not remember those days."

"Only a very little," said Odette. "And what my father told me about Saint Domingue and this plantation. Some of what I think of as memories no doubt were from his stories. Why do you ask?"

"I was present in the house the night you were born," the servant said steadily. "Your sainted mother was in labor for two days prior to your arrival and everyone knew, your mother included, that she would die in childbirth, and perhaps you with her."

Odette nodded. Her father had told her this story many times, causing much guilt in Odette. If she had never been born would her mother still be alive today? It seemed odd that Jacques should be bringing up this old memory so many years later, and on the very date of her birthday. Perhaps it was just this date that had made him remember.

"Your mother had called for both the family lawyer and for the priest," Jacques said slowly. "She knew her immortal soul was in peril if she did not receive absolution before passing from this life to the next. And the sin which weighed on her soul was so great she wished to make arrangements in this world for you as well."

"For me?" Odette was surprised.

"Yes, for you. She left a letter in my hands, which had been prepared by the lawyer, to be given you on this very day, should I still be alive. I have kept the letter safe all this time, with no belief I would ever see you again, or be obliged to deliver the letter. But this day has come and we are together, so deliver it I must."

"And do you know the contents of this letter?"

"Yes, Madame, I do. The lawyer bid me read the contents before sealing it up, which I did. I often wish I had never been made privy to its contents."

"Well, Jacques, what a mystery!" exclaimed Odette. "Shall I open it now?"

"No, Madame, I would wish you open it before you go to bed tonight, Enjoy your party first, then the letter. I am afraid it is going to change your life.

"Goodness! How solemn you sound, Jacques. Well, I will obey your wishes. Will you give me the letter now?

"Not until after the party, Madame, then you take it upstairs and open it. Remember it has been sealed these twenty one years." He bowed deeply and withdrew, leaving Odette fervently wishing Jacques had never mentioned such a letter, wondering what it could possibly contain. There was little time for speculation. It was time to go upstairs and dress for the evening ahead.

In their chamber Odette found her husband, sprawled out on their bed. She prayed he would not want to make sexual use of her before the dinner and gala entertainment planned for afterward. It was enough to dress and be downstairs on time in this hot and heavy weather without performing gymnastics on the bed and becoming even more sticky and hot. Fortunately, Boucher showed no signs of sexual interest. Indeed, when she glanced over at him she saw he looked extremely unwell. He was sweating even more than usual, which would make his donning of formal clothes for the evening make his smell even more rank than usual. Perhaps she could stay far away from him among the other guests. His face was drawn and somehow gray and he clenched and unclenched his fists, scrunching up the bedcover in his large paws.

"Are you unwell?" she asked as kindly as she could.

"Just another bout of biliousness," he muttered through clenched teeth.

"I hope you are well enough to join in the festivities tonight," Odette murmured.

"No fear, I will be there." Boucher managed to get to his feet and call for his valet, who helped him into the adjoining dressing room, leaving Odette free in the shared bedchamber to make her own preparations. She called the housemaid, Eulalie, who was brilliant at hair dressing, and settled down at her dressing table for the woman to curl and braid her hair into the latest French fashion, before donning the sheer, high waisted gown in palest blue she had selected as appropriate wear for her party. A knock at the door brought Pauline herself into the room, already dressed in silver tissue, bands of which were intertwined with white roses in her hair.

"I only wanted to wish you well and bring you this," she indicated a charming bouquet of roses to match her head ornaments, which she lay on the dressing table.

"Thank you Madame," said Odette. "It is too kind of you to give me this grand party tonight."

"It is nothing," Pauline told her. "And it is a most special occasion. I am so glad to have a reason for the musicians to perform and for cook to produce a splendid repast. We have it written out on several menu cards, which are placed at intervals on the tables. And the flowers! They are heaven on earth. Just wait until you see." She dropped a light kiss onto Odette's curls and left the room. Odette heard her trip lightly down the stairs - which she was quite able to do when the mood took her – and call for Jacques in the downstairs hall.

The memory of Jacques and the mysterious letter came to the forefront of her mind, but she resolutely put it aside. The letter would arrive when Jacques thought the time was ripe. In the meantime, it was her responsibility to dress and be downstairs in time to receive the guests with Pauline. She turned to the glass, watching Eulalie perform her magic.

And magic it was, from the moment the first officer arrived, striding up the verandah steps importantly, bowing before the two ladies who stood side by side in the front hall. A line of other guests followed shortly behind, and all were directed through the house to the fragrant garden behind, where round tables of eight had been set up for dining. Pauline's mulatto orchestra were in perfect tune, playing one melody after another, whose notes floated out and up in the tropical air.

Servants circulated with trays of champagne flutes, interspersed with drinks of the tropical fruits that so abounded on the island.

The last guest had made his appearance and gone through the formalities of greeting his hostess and the guest of honor before Boucher came clumping down the stairs. He had managed to squeeze into a formal coat of heavy brocade, satin knee britches and fine slippers of softest Spanish leather, but he looked as unwell as he had upstairs. Odette decided to ignore any signs of illness; if Boucher felt he was well enough to attend the party, so be it. She would not cross him in this for it might well provoke an argument which would ruin the party. She simply followed Pauline out to the garden, where they joined the throng of guests, drinking happily under the strings of Japanese lanterns strung through the trees, augmented by scores of candles lighting the dinner tables.

Dinner was announced shortly thereafter and the guests sought their places, settling in with pleasure. As Pauline had said, there were menu cards scattered over the tables, which listed the dishes that would constitute the meal they were about to partake of. These had been carefully written out by Jacques, and read as follows:

Ecrevesses grille au citron

~

Tortue Claire

~

Canard a l'orange

~

Navarin d'agneau avec les legumes tropicale

~

Pommes Duchesse, Petit pois a la Anglaise. Asperges mousseline,
Coeurs de Romaine

~

Compote des fruits
Macarons
Mille Feuilles

~

'Nog Odette'

Each course was borne out by a phalanx of white gloved waiters,
who had been trained to help the guests with pairs of serving pieces as
carefully as if they had been back in Paris in the Tuilleries Palace. As
dish followed dish, each with its accompanying wine, or the special 'nog'
invented by the cook in honor of Odette's birthday, conversation became
more animated. Many a sexual innuendo passed between the men and
women seated at the tables in the garden, many an assignation was
arranged for later in the evening. When the compote was borne out, on
an enormous silver platter, it was festooned and garlanded with swirls
of perfectly spun sugar, and earned a round of applause from the guests.
Pauline noted to herself that a large tip to the chef would be in order.

Down in the fields beyond the house, the French troops, too,
were having their own celebration, with roast goat and the rice and bean
dish so typical of the cuisine on San Domingue. They washed down their
repast with raw rum, produced on the estate, and there was many a sore
head on the morrow. Further away from the house, the black plantation
workers were also celebrating, with their own roast goats and dancing
to the throbbing tempo of jungle drums.

Everyone but Boucher seemed to be having a wonderful time.
Odette glanced at him from time to time, seated as he was directly across

the table from her, between the next door planter's buxom wife and General Leclerc's aide de camp, Major Montreux. The two were in animated conversation across Boucher, who slumped in his chair, not touching a drop or a crumb. Odette decided to ignore the situation for as long as she could. If her husband was becoming ill then no doubt she would have days ahead to nurse him. Right now she was enjoying being the center of attention at this charming event.

After dinner the chairs were pushed back and the orchestra began to play dance music. Almost all the guests took to the floor, erected in the middle of the garden for this purpose. Boucher, however, remained slumped in his chair and so alarmed Odette with his lack of any interest in the party went over to him to inquire if he wished to be helped upstairs. She was greeted with a blank stare and a terse 'Do not concern yourself with me. It would be disrespectful to our hostess."

Pauline, out on the floor with a young Lieutenant, who was holding her much too tightly for decorum's sake, was far beyond any concern for her guests. She had done her part and was now going to enjoy herself. The young man whispered something into her ear and she gazed up at him, adoringly, giving her tinkling laugh.

Colonel Duval bowed before her. "May I have the honor?" He held out his hand and Odette took it, allowing him to lead her out amid the other dancers, He circled her waist with his arm and commenced twirling her around the floor, swooping to the music.

Surely this was as close to heaven as she would ever come on earth. Odette leaned into his embrace, forgetting her resolve to keep this man – literally – at arm's length. Tonight was hers and tomorrow she would come back down to reality again.

On and on the musicians played into the tropical night, on and on the dancers swung and swooped across the floor, some pairs disappearing into the welcoming shadows at the sides of the garden. Later they would slip back among the dancers and who could say how they whiled away the minutes among the overhanging fronds of palm and the swinging garlands of tropical flowers, growing in such profusion

105

as to make a screen to shield the little amors taking place so close to the dance floor?

It was well past midnight when the last dance came to a close, the musicians stopped playing and the final guest took his departure, kissing the hands of both Odette and Pauline. The two couples, Leclercs and Bouchers, stood once again in the front hall.

"Madame, I cannot thank you enough for such a delightful evening," Odette said to Pauline.

"Zut! It was fun for me too. Now get you two to bed and I do not expect to see either of you before lunch tomorrow. I intend to sleep and sleep and sleep. She took her husband by the hand and pulled him up the stairs behind her. Their door shut and for once there was silence. The party had gone on so long as to shut down even Pauline's sexual desires. No doubt they would once again surface with the dawn, but for now the house was quiet.

Odette started up the stairs with Boucher lumbering clumsily behind her. They entered their bedchamber where he managed to stagger across the room to the bed and fall face down upon it."

"I feel dreadful," he muttered, so low his wife could barely hear him.

"Let me call your valet to undress you and get you to bed. Perhaps I will sleep in your dressing room, so as not to disturb you. I will be able to hear though in case you need me in the night."

Boucher reached out a hand for hers. "Don't go, "he muttered thickly. "Sick, so sick." He managed to prop himself up on one elbow and was violently sick all over the bed covers, spewing up noxious amounts of vomit tinged with blood.

Odette recoiled, both from the smell and from the blood. "Oh, husband, what is it?" She cried.

He fell back on the bed and now she saw that terrifying sign of the dreaded fever, his skin, shrunken somehow and unmistakably yellow.

106

She sent the fan boy running for Jacques, to send for the plantation doctor, otherwise the vet, who was in charge of treating the human patients who worked on the plantation. His services were deemed good enough for the blacks, whose worth was probably less per capita than the fine horses and hunting dogs belonging to the French officers.

The man appeared, wide eyed, a quarter of an hour later. He had not expected to be called to the big house to treat any of the white inhabitants there; they would usually send to Le Cap for the head army doctor instead. Tonight, however, was an exception and there was no one else.

Even though he was mainly a doctor to the animals, there was no mistaking the early signs of the dreaded Siamese Fever, which had already felled so many of the French army.

"Madame," he stammered to Odette. "While it is the fever, some people do recover from it. However, in case it is the more virulent form, the General should be moved from the house, the better to avoid contamination for anyone here. I will have a litter prepared and he can be taken to the workers' hospital beyond the cabins. There I will tend to him myself, while you and the General and his wife and child remain relatively safe here."

"No, "said Odette steadily. "My place is by his side and I will accompany him there and nurse him myself. It is my duty." She went behind the screen in the corner of the room and hastily dressed herself, pulling off her evening finery carelessly and dropping the exquisite garments to the floor. She pulled on her simplest day dress, caught up a shawl and left her hair in its ringlets, curls and braids. It was too complicated for her to take down in any case, and would only waste time. She followed the litter with her sick husband groaning on it down the wide staircase, out across the verandah and into the night, where so recently she and the guests had dined and danced.

Lying on the dressing table, in the room so recently vacated by Bouchers, was a thick envelope, yellowed with age and curling around the edges, unnoticed and forgotten in the haste to remove Boucher from the house. It was the document, so carefully described by Jacques to Odette only days before. In light of the terrible development of contracting the dread fever, no one had noticed it.

Chapter Six

Widowed

Boucher lingered three days in a screened off corner of the hospital, where lay so many of the French soldiers whom he had commanded these past months on the island. Most were ill of the fever, and very few were expected to survive.

Odette kept vigil at his bedside, until, on the second day without sleep or indeed any rest, she simply collapsed, sliding to the floor from the hard wooden chair beside her husband's bed. An orderly picked her up and sent a messenger post haste to the house. Several house servants cam running, proceeded by Jacques, and her inert form was loaded on a stretcher for transport back up the hill to the big house where she was put to bed. The room had been washed down with a solution of vinegar and water, against the possible infection, but the inhabitants of the house had been exposed to the fever so often as to make any sort of quarantine superfluous. All of them had, at some time in the past months, experienced slight bouts of the dread disease, and all had recovered. Boucher, it seemed, would break this record and he did, dying on the third day as dawn broke in the sky, while his wife still lay white and wan in what had been their matrimonial bed.

Boucher was buried with full military honors in the family cemetery of his in laws, by sunset of the same day he died. It was not prudent to keep bodies unburied longer in the tropical climate, and there was no hope of embalming the corpse, sealing it in a lead coffin and waiting for transport to France. Too many of the French had died to observe these niceties, so speed burial was the order of the day.

Odette managed to rally enough to attend the ceremony, flanked by Leclerc's strong arm on one side and Duval's on the other. Pauline, ever loath to walk farther than she must, was carried on a litter which was placed beside her husband. Her band played the Marseilles only missing a few of the higher notes, and a six gun salute to the fallen general echoed over the valley, rebounding from the blue hills in the distance. The Leclercs and Odette repaired to the house for a cold collation. Duval hovered at a respectful distance from the verandah steps, until Pauline waved her hand at him.

Join us, Colonel," she trilled. "You are practically a member of the family as you have been with us so long, guarding us from any marauders who might venture onto the property."

The colonel mounted the steps and took the wicker chair next to Odette. She motioned to one of the servants, who sprang forward to pour a glass of white wine for Duval, which he took stiffly, not even sipping it.

"It is a sad business, this," said Leclerc. "When such an able soldier falls, not in battle, but to a terrible illness that we cannot seem to escape. I do not know how any of us here have avoided contracting the more virulent form of it before now."

Pauline actually crossed herself. "Oh, Charles," she exclaimed, "do not court fate by mentioning our good luck. It surely will change, and not for the better." She looked so distressed her husband put his hand over hers.

"Tut, Madame. Such superstitions would be more in keeping with the voodoo practiced on this island than among civilized people. "

Pauline seemed only slightly mollified. She made a moue with her mouth, then took two large gulps of the wine, which seemed to refresh her. Realizing she needed to say something comforting to Odette, she turned to her lady in waiting.

"Have no fear," she said, "that we will not take care of you in your distress. You always have a home with us, and I hope you will continue in my service as long as it suits you. We will all be going home to France one of these days, where I will do my utmost to find a suitable second husband for you." She apparently did not realize what she had said, for she continued on, undaunted, "my brother, Napoleon, will no doubt want to grant you a widow's pension commensurate with your husband's position in the army," she trilled on, "and there is a family chateau, somewhere near Lyons I believe?"

"It is no longer family property," Odette said so low Pauline had to strain to hear her. "It was confiscated by the revolutionary forces."

"Then I will influence Napoleon to get it back for you," Pauline promised rashly. "It is the least he can do after the service shown me and my husband by both you and your husband."

Next to her Leclerc was clearly shaking his head, trying to stop his wife from making any more rash promises. She, however, did not notice and continued on with her thoughts.

"But of course you have this plantation, too," she said gaily. "Though I cannot imagine you wanting to stay out here on this godforsaken island when we return to France..." she finally trailed off, noticing the furious expression on her husband's face.

"It is the island of my birth," Odette said slowly, "and I find many things of beauty here. And I have no family left in France. My aunt died before we came out here and, as you know, my father lost his head a month after the Queen."

"Ah, yes, you aristocrats!" Pauline exclaimed. "Well, when the time comes it is your decision to make."

"Indeed it is," seconded Leclerc. "And now perhaps Madame would like to retire to her room. Surely the day has been wearing enough and you would like to rest?"

"Thank you," said Odette gratefully. "I *am* tired. I think I will go upstairs."

Duval jumped to his feet, holding her chair for her to rise, then bowed to Odette. "Madame, my deepest sympathies on your great loss. If I can be of any help to you n the future, please do not hesitate to call on me." He escorted her across the verandah and into the front hall, then watched as, wearily, she climbed the stairs to the room she had so recently shared with Boucher.

Two candles burned softly in the room, one on the dressing table, one on a small table beside the bed. She hastened to strike a light and held it to the wick of the several other candles in the room, illuminating even the shadowy corners of the chamber. She wondered if she would be able to sleep in this bed so lately shared with her husband, now dead and buried in the cemetery that held many of his in-laws. What would he think, buried so far away from France, among strangers. Well, maybe once dead he no longer had to concern himself with such earthly arrangements. Devoutedly she hoped so.

Odette sank down on the stool at the dressing table, and examined her reflection in the streaky mirror. She saw a familiar face staring back at her, eyes smudged underneath with circles of tiredness, limp, lackluster hair, mouth turned down. But it was still Odette. She squared her shoulders. She had been a soldier's wife, and she had never wavered in her duties to her husband, however distasteful they had become. He was gone but she was still here with much of her life still ahead of her. She would survive.

A yellowing envelope, placed in the exact center of the dressing table, caught her attention. The letter Jacques had mentioned...was it really only a few days ago? The letter he had promised her on her twenty first birthday.

Taking a large hairpin from her elaborate coiffure, she carefully slit the envelope, careful not to destroy it or its contents. She drew the damp sheets carefully out, mindful that these pages had survived over two decades in a climate that could easily destroy almost everything it touched. She smoothed out the contents of the envelope, and drew a five branched candelabra nearer to her, the better to read the letter.

Old fashioned spiky writing, fashionable during the days of the ancient regime leaped up at her.

'The following is at the dictation of Mme. La Comtesse du Soissons, this Seventeenth Day of May, in the year of our Lord, Seventeen Hundred and Eighty two:

To my dearest daughter:

I hold you in my arms for the first and last time, for I know I am dying and do not have much more time to live. I am heartbroken that I will not be here to see you grow up, to become a woman, to love and guide you on your way. I do not even know if you will remain in the land of your birth, or travel with my husband back to his home in France. None of this will be in my hands, but in the hands of Marcel Levallier, Comte du Soissons. You may well ask, my daughter, why I do not refer to my husband as your father. This is because he is not; another man fathered you, which fact I have decided to hide from you until you are twenty one. If then you can be reached, I am asking that Jacques, my major domo, be responsible for getting this missive to you.

My husband was much away from the plantation during the years of our marriage, traveling to Cuba and France on business connected with the selling of our sugar cane crops and the products derived from this: rum and refined sugar, as well as molasses and the cane itself. Many months I have been alone here, with only the servants for company and my own thoughts. I have taught the slave, Jacques, to read and write, which is illegal and for which I could be punished severely by the authorities. But he has proved an eager and an intelligent pupil and, during the course of our lessons, I have become much attached to him. So much, indeed, that I have come to love him, not as a mistress loves her servant, but as a woman loves a man. A year ago my husband undertook a sea voyage to France, promising to return when he had completed necessary business there. During that time I succumbed to the charms of Jacques, and we consummated our love for one another. I am not proud of what I did, but the loneliness and the isolation here on the plantation so wore me down I came to welcome his caresses. Two months before my husband's return, I discovered I was with child and had no idea what to do. After much anguish, I decided to say nothing of my condition, and would pretend that the child – you – was the fruit of my marriage to Marcel. I prayed your birth would not come early, and that you would be a small baby, one I could claim was premature. Such has come to pass for you are a small child, though perfectly formed and certainly full term.

I could not die with such a sin on my conscience, and will be making full confession to Pere Lachamps, who is even now at my bedside. I hope God will forgive me. And you, too, my perfect, beautiful child. God bless you and hold you forever in the palm of his hand.

Your loving mother, Celestine

A footnote appeared at the end of this astonishing missive:

"Mme. La Comtesse confessed her sins to the Priest and was granted absolution. She died a scarce hour later, leaving the baby Odette an orphan, but as neither I nor the Priest will break the seal of silence as observed by our separate professions, I cannot give this information to M. Le Comte, who will now accept this baby as his own. A copy of this letter will remain in my possession and a copy given to the major domo, Jacques. Whether or not it will ever be delivered to the baby daughter of La Comtesse is in the hands of fate.

A scrawled signature completed the pages Odette now held in her hand, pages which fell to the floor as her fingers opened involuntarily.

It was almost more than she could take in: first the death of her husband, now the knowledge that her whole life had been lived as the result of a lie. Her father not her father! Her father was Jacques! The relatives who had nurtured and sheltered her in France were actually no relations at all. Her mother had committed adultery and her father had been duped into believing the daughter, born twenty one years ago, was his own. And, while her real father, Jacques, bore some part of white blood in his veins, he still passed his Negro blood to her, making her a quadroon or an octoroon.

The exhaustion of the past few days, coupled with this monstrous letter from beyond the grave, sent Odette toppling over to her bed, where she passed out cold, fully dressed, across the coverlet.

The slant of morning light fell across her inert body, waking Odette from the fitful slumber she had experienced during the night. She sat up groggily, with a head that felt like it was stuffed with cotton wool, a bad headache and a mouth so parched she was unable to find her voice. She pulled the bell cord to summon the maid for an early morning cup of coffee. Perhaps it would waken her fully. Perhaps last night had been nothing but a dream, fervently felt at the time but dissipating to nothingness in the early sunlight. But no, such was not the case. Odette peered over the side of the bed to see the crumpled sheets of the lawyer's letter lying on the floor. She reached down to catch them up, lost her balance, and fell heavily onto the bare floor boards. The maid, Claude, entered a moment later and raised the alarm, followed closely by Pauline who had pulled a light peignoir hastily over her nakedness. The garment barely covered her, making her ever the more sensuous looking than if she had stood fully nude beside Odette's bed.

"What has happened? Are you alright? What can I do?" She blurted out these sentences so fast as to be practically gibberish, but the kindness of her meaning shone through the garbled words. Odette could only lie and stare up at the concerned face above her.

Soon footsteps were pounding down the corridor as several men servant's rushed to Odette's aid, scooped her up and placed her back on her bed. Pauline shooed them all out of the room, overlooking of course the small boy in the corner who still plied his string to move the overhead fan.

The maid turned to Pauline and sketched a small curtsey. "Please, Madame, return to your chamber while I attend to Mme. Boucher; I will send word as soon as I have her settled.

Pauline planted a gentle kiss on her lady in waiting's forehead and soundlessly left the room.

Gently the maid undressed her mistress, taking up a sponge soaked in cool water and bathing the body all over, tut-tutting about the bruises that even now were appearing as a consequence of the fall. She brushed Odette's hair, tied it back with a red ribbon and slipped a clean starched nightdress over her head. She straightened the bedclothes as best she could with Odette lying on them, then went out to order coffee and warm rolls, hoping to revive her mistress.

Odette sank back against the bolsters and pillows and willed her mind to stop chuttering around in ever faster and smaller circles. How had so much happened in the course of only a few days? Where was she now and where was she going? Nothing seemed clear, all was hazy and confused. She watched the blades of the fan rotate gently above her, barely moving the humid air that even at this early hour was becoming almost unbearable.

The maid forced some coffee and a bit of roll down Odette's throat, then smoothed the light sheet over her body and stepped back from the bed.

"Rest now, Madame," she intoned gently. "Perhaps when you do you will feel better." She turned and went out the door, leaving Odette to her thoughts.

Never had a day passed more slowly, or more agonizingly. Dimly she heard the sounds of the household all around her: the jangle of horses' bridles under her window on the drive, the chatter of the servants as they went about their duties, cleaning and dusting and polishing. She heard Leclerc's boots on the stairs, shortly followed by Pauline's much lighter slippers, the silence on the upper floor. Insects chirped and birds sang, the sun passed from east to west, bringing a slightly cooler temperature, and still Odette lay, not caring about any of it.

Dusk fell and she made a supreme effort to sit up in the bed. She could not lie forever in a stupor, in spite of all that had befallen. She rang again for Claude and insisted on being dressed and helped down to the small drawing room where she hoped to find Pauline. Surely her employer deserved an explanation for her companion's total collapse. How hard it would be to give this explanation, but it was necessary she do so.

A half hour later, supported on the stairs by the ever faithful maid, Odette tottered to the first floor and across the wide boards of the hallway into the small salon where it was customary to meet before dinner.

Pauline was indeed there before her, her feet on a male servant whom she was using for a footstool. Another stood behind her back, fanning her with a huge fan made of brilliant feathers. She was dressed in a gown so low cut her breasts all but bobbed out of the skimpy muslin and she looked absolutely enchanting. The two ladies were joined almost immediately by Leclerc and, to Odette's dismay, Duval, who immediately came to her side and lifted her limp hand to kiss.

Odette stiffened her spine and confessed to the company that she was not who she thought she was all her life; she was not the daughter of the Count de Soissons, but of a black worker on the estate and the mother she had never known. She spoke as plainly as she possibly could, not mincing her words. She believed this revelation would not only lose her the position as Pauline's lady in waiting, but would probably put her outside the bounds of polite society as well. Her announcement met with stunned silence for a moment, then the three others in the room all spoke at once.

From Leclerc: "Madame, I find it hard to believe...."

Pauline: "My poor, poor friend...."

But Duval's remark made her lift her head again, and give him a long, level look: "It makes absolutely no difference to me, Madame. You are what you have always been, a true lady of refinement and delicacy." He lifted her hand once more and brought it to his lips.

A tiny ray of hope blossomed in Odette's troubled breast. Would these three, her closest allies in this land of her birth, actually accept what she had just told them without passing judgment on her?

Pauline continued. "None of this is your fault, and none of it need matter. Do you know who the man was who fathered you?"

Odette dropped her eyes and lied, "No, Madame, my mother did not say in her letter." She had decided to shield Jacques in this matter, not knowing what the penalty might be for the act he had committed in this very house twenty one years ago.

"Then it is something that will never be known," said Leclerc. "But the fact may work to our advantage."

"Our advantage?" Pauline queried.

"Yes, when dealing with the rebels. They have looked at us as the outsiders ever since we came to this god-forsaken island only months ago. But now we have an ally in our midst, one who fuses the best of both worlds within her person." He stared at Odette. "Duval, we must contemplate how best to use this new information to our advantage. And now, ladies, let us go in to dinner. We will discuss this later, while you are having coffee after the meal.

The general had spoken and the others had but to obey. Leclerc offered his arm to Pauline and led her through the double doors into the white paneled dining room, where the table was set, as usual, with a plethora of silver, fine china and glass and blazing candelabra that only added to the heat of the tropical night. Duval followed with Odette on his arm and the four settled down to a heavy meal of five courses each with its accompanying wine.

The men's talk turned to the events of the ongoing rebellion. Many of the black officers who had so recently sworn allegiance to France, were even now creeping off again to join the rebels up in the hills, taking their men with them. Leclerc had ordered the execution of thirty of these officers, those he could find, which had angered the black population greatly. That, coupled with the recent arrest and deportation of L'Ouverture to prison in France had turned the tide of war again against the French conquerors, and Leclerc was hard pressed to keep order on the island. The relief troops he had requested from Napoleon had been long in coming and short of the number he had requested, some twelve thousand only had arrived out of the thirty thousand he needed. And half of them died shortly after landing, of the dreaded Siamese fever and other tropical diseases. It was indeed a dire situation faced by the remaining French troops and their officers.

"The only way to continue to keep order on this island," bellowed Leclerc, "is to kill almost all of the black population. Only then will we be safe from a massacre." He pounded his fist so hard on the table as to cause his wine glass to topple over, leaving a long puddle of blood-red all over the white cloth. Servants sprang forward to mop up the spill and cover the stain with fresh napkins, but no one at the table could help but compare the red tide with the blood so far spilled in the name of France, or the blood that would no doubt be spilled in the future.

Leclerc continued: "The only solution as I see it is to kill the majority of the free blacks on this island, including the women and children. We are so far outnumbered by these that I fear we will never be able to cement the hold we now have. The black tides will sweep over us and annihilate us all given time."

Duval looked perplexed. "Surely all the free blacks can't be against us?" he protested.

"I think they are," Leclerc replied in a more normal tone. "They feel it is their island and we are here to wrest it from them..."

"Which is truly the case," Duval interjected.

"We secure the island for France," Leclerc answered stiffly. "And what is worse, ever since the sale of slaves has been reintroduced in Guadeloupe, the peoples of San Domingue have greatly feared the same thing will happen here. I have given orders to shoot anyone who is not loyal to France, to shoot on sight." He gestured for Jacques to pour more wine into his glass, which had been righted by a hovering waiter.

The black servants all kept their faces impassive during this diatribe, as if the events described by the French general had no impact on their lives. Might they, too, be shot for treason? Was anyone, black or white, safe on the island? At least Jacques, who had been listening at the salon door, knew that his participation in Odette's conception would never be revealed by the young woman, his own beautiful daughter, whom he could never acknowledge but only love and worship from afar.

The meal progressed, uneasily, to its close, at which point the ladies rose to leave the men alone. Duval leaped to his feet to help the ladies from their chairs, but Leclerc remained seated, taking deep draughts of his wine. His face was flushed and Duval feared he would not be coherent while discussing the future plans for the securing and holding of the island. He sighed; perhaps these plans could be saved for the morning. He returned to his seat, taking up his own glass and eyeing the commander warily. Leclerc rarely drank too much; the present situation together with Odette's astonishing revelation must have proved too much for one evening.

Shortly the general lumbered to his feet, crashing his chair over behind him. "I seek respite from the terrible events that daily occupy my whole being," he announced in a thick voice. "Tonight I will cease my campaigning and retire with my wife early."

Duval bowed the general out of the room and into the small salon.

"Wife," commanded Leclerc, "accompany me to our chamber. I would retire now." He held out his hand, which Pauline grasped happily, allowing one rounded breast to actually rise from his moorings and bob above the neckline of her gown.

"With pleasure." she simpered.

Her husband draped his arm around his wife's shoulder, letting his fingers linger on the tempting breast, taking the rosy nipple between his thumb and forefinger. "I long for surcease."

"Which I am happy to provide." Pauline led Leclerc out of the room and together they ascended the stairs, from where Odette and

Duval could hear giggles from Pauline and the distinct sound of sucking. The upstairs door closed and almost immediately the bed commenced to squeak and wail, the headboard pounding rhythmically against the wall as the Leclercs' began their almost nightly session of hot, lengthy sex.

Left in the small salon together, Odette and Duval could but pretend they did not hear the unmistakable sounds from above. They glanced away from each other, embarrassed at being left alone in such close proximity. At length Duval broke the silence.

"You must know, Madame," he began tentatively, "that I have admired you for many months, ever since we took ship together last December from France. I am sorry I so forgot myself a few months ago in the wood, it was inexcusable for me, especially as I could see you would never in any way betray your husband. And I want you to know to know that your mixed blood no way detracts from my admiration of you. Indeed it seems to enhance it for it makes you more at one with this island which I am coming to love."

Odette turned to him, her eyes full of tears. "But, Colonel," she said so low he had to strain to hear her. "The respect I demonstrated was not due to any love for my husband; far from it. It was from nothing more than a sense of duty: he had married me, made me his own, when I was a girl of seventeen, and I had never known any other man but him. It was an arranged marriage and I went to him directly from the convent school where I was placed by my father. The nuns had repeated over and over until their teachings became a part of us that we owed total loyalty to our husbands. That adultery was a mortal sin, punishable by eternal damnation. I thought he would be kind to me, kind and gentle in matters of..." she paused, embarrassed to go on. "Intimacy. Between a husband and wife." She lowered her eyes, so as not to have to look at him. "But he was not kind, or gentle, yet still I believed I owed him my total allegiance, as my husband."

Duval was not surprised at this admission. Around the officers' mess Boucher was known to use and abuse the camp followers who were an ever present part of any army. Duval was only devastated to know that the man had treated his gently reared wife like the lowest trollop. He clenched his teeth as the knowledge sunk in and, inadvertently, took up Odette's hand again.

"I am here to serve you, Madame, in any way you wish to use me. Please believe my undying devotion to you, which I can now declare, since you no longer have a husband." He turned her hand over and kissed the palm, his warm breath sending a small sensation of pleasure to melt the troubled heart of Odette. For the first time in days she relaxed, enjoying the attentions of this handsome man, drinking in the scent of his hair, his breath, tinged with brandy and cigars, the very maleness of his body which was so close to her own. He encircled her with his arm and she leaned, gratefully, into the safety of his embrace.

They did not kiss, there was no impropriety between them, it was as if each had weathered a storm and had now come, at long last, into a safe harbor.

They remained thus joined for the next half hour, while the moon rose and the noises from above ceased. The cicadas continued their loud chorus out in the garden and the scent of roses and frangipani drifted through the open French doors. It was with regret that Odette pulled away from Boucher and rose from the loveseat. He immediately was on his feet, offering her his arm, which she took, fingers lightly resting on the satin of his sleeve. He ushered her to the foot of the stairs, where he once again took her hand, kissed it and stepped back. He watched her graceful gait as she ascended to the second floor and passed from view. He stood there for a moment longer, savoring the scent of her perfume and thinking on the half hour just passed, one that promised to change his life entirely in the days to come.

The next morning Odette was almost back to her normal self, and Leclerc announced that the household was returning to the Governor's Residence in Le Cap. He had need of the loyalty of the citizens of the town, to fight against the inevitable uprising he was sure would come, and come soon. He wrote Napoleon that only with complete mastery of the island native population by the French invaders would secure San Domingue for France. With each passing day, as more and more native troops returned to the rebel forces, this hope became dimmer and dimmer. Leclerc's dream of a glorious victory, accomplished through diplomacy rather than bloodshed was fast fading from view. Instead, he was faced with total failure of the mission. But still he pressed on, hoping against hope to overcome the rebels and gain lasting peace.

Down in the town, Duval had more duties to perform for his Commander in Chief, and was often absent, thus having little time to devote to Odette. She bore this with patience, trusting that his words in the dim light of the salon were true, that he meant that he would be her champion and – someday, she hoped – her love.

Pauline instantly noticed the new glow that had come to her lady in waiting, and put it down to the one emotion she knew best: love. She wished to help Odette know the true joys of sex and set about trying to educate her on the best way to experience the rapture she herself attained – with so many different men.

Seated on the veranda of the Residence, which overlooked the port of Le Cap and the many vessels bobbing on its waters, Pauline introduced topics about which Odette knew nothing.

"You must be seductive, ma petite," she told Odette one morning, as the two ladies lounged on a shaded corner of the verandah. Pauline was reclining in the hammock slung from two porch pillars, while Odette sat on a low ottoman at her feet, stitching on a piece of embroidery. "You must learn to emphasize your good points, and hide, if necessary, your not so good ones." She looked the other woman over critically. "For example, you bind your breasts too tightly. They should be untrammeled, easy to lift from your bodice. You should also rouge the nipples, as I do." She let the peignoir she wore fall open, to reveal nothing underneath. "It is advisable to be available to your lover at all times, as I am now. A man can simply reach inside these folds..." she pulled back the thin chiffon which barely covered her charms, "and take what he wants." She emitted a short laugh, as she stroked her breasts, letting her hand travel down lower on her body, to cover the black muff of hair between her legs. "It is rarely necessary to encourage him," she continued dreamily. "The sight of a woman's body is enough to stiffen his prick, to get him ready for the act of sexual congress. Of course, when he is ready you may not necessarily be so. Though usually I am," she added softly, commencing to stroke her plump white thighs. A low moan escaped her lips.

This time, Odette listened closely. Would she finally understand just what it was between a man and a woman which caused so much pleasurable chaos? Which led to heights of rapture about which she could only guess? If it was too soon after her husband's death for such thoughts, well, tant pis. She had given him all she had for the previous four years, enduring hours of unpleasantness and even downright pain. Now he was gone, her time was coming and she intended to enjoy it to the full.

She leaned eagerly toward Pauline, willing her to go on.

Pauline seemed far away, but managed to pull herself back to go on with her lesson in the arts of love.

"Where was I? Oh, the readiness for the joining of our bodies. If the woman is not ready for the insertion of the man's fully engaged member into the tenderest part of her body, then he must help her. There are several ways he can do this. He can insert his finger inside her, at the same time rubbing the nub of all pleasure between her legs. This almost always produces enough fluid to make the insertion of him pleasurable. Or, he can use his lips to suck and his tongue in the place of his finger. This causes the most intense kind of pleasure for the woman – for the man too, come to think of it. All is in an effort to make the insertion of him into her with the most passion and the most feeling possible. You know, of course, that there are various positions taken by both the man and woman to attain this?" She regarded Odette sharply.

"Yes, I know," murmured Odette. "But how can such insertion be pleasurable to the woman?"

"Huh," snorted Pauline. "I can see your Boucher had no finesse in such matters. He just pushed and shoved into you, didn't he? Which caused you nothing but pain?"

"I fear it was so," said Odette.

"Well, rest assured, Duval will no doubt prove the perfect lover, particularly if you let him know what it is that pleasures you the most. He will then perform to make you happy, as you will make him."

Odette blushed to the roots of her hair. "Oh, Madame! How could I be so lascivious?"

Pauline chuckled. "You will surprise yourself with what you can ask for when in the throes of desire. And often the more lewd the request, the more your lover is excited by you. But I have not told you of the various ways in which a man can enter you. Have you any knowledge of this?"

"A little," Odette replied. "But, truly, none was to my liking."

"That is no doubt because your husband did not intend them to be," said Pauline. "Some men simply do not care if a woman experiences any pleasure in the sexual act, others because they only care about themselves."

"But the nuns told us..." Odette began.

"Nuns!" scoffed Pauline. "And what did they know? Absolutely nothing. They were the last women who should have been trying to educate young women in the art of love. Our mothers took the same route: tell us absolutely nothing and let us find out on our wedding night! I found out long before my wedding night, let me tell you. And I have been finding out more and more as time goes on. I only hope you will too, and soon." She lay back on her cushions, breathing hard. "Now I think I wish to return to my room to rest for a bit before luncheon. Will you send one of the servants to find Leclerc and ask him to join me? He was looking somewhat tired himself this morning." She rose and languidly drifted across the porch toward the wide front hall and the staircase.

Smiling inwardly, Odette rose to summon a servant. Rest indeed! She knew what Pauline would be doing shortly and with whom. When Leclerc was at home, he obeyed his wife's invitations to join her in their chamber instantly. When he was in the field then someone else would be summoned in his place.

Odette returned to her seat, feeling even hotter than usual. Surely the temperature had not risen in the hour or so she and Pauline had been talking? Her breath, too, seemed to be coming in shorter and shorter; indeed, she was almost panting. She rose again and took the hammock so recently vacated by her mistress, flinging herself out its length and sinking into the pile of pillows at her head. A rope strung through the lattice was at hand, and she pulled it gently, rocking to and fro. Thoughts rolled around in her head, thoughts of a handsome Colonel whose lips had so recently kissed her palm. What if those lips were to kiss other parts of her body, starting with her lips, pursed now as if to receive that kiss? She was ripe and ready to discover what she had been missing all these years.

An hour later she met Leclerc and Pauline at the lunch table. The Governor was, as usual, buttoned and buckled neatly into his uniform, the only sign of the recent sexual romp was a certain sweatiness to his hair, a glazed gleam in his eye. Pauline, on the other hand, appeared delightfully disheveled, with curls askew in her elaborate coiffure, red patches on the low cut neckline of her frock, where no doubt she had been scratched by her husband's whiskers. She entered the dining room with an uncertain gait, moving slowly and carefully, and settled carefully into the thick padding of her chair. No doubt she had been well and thoroughly reamed by her husband, for a lengthy period of time, and was feeling the effects.

Odette wondered how it would feel to her to have her nether parts so well pounded by the engorged prick of a man who excited her, who pleasured her, who satisfied her? She twitched in her chair, nervy and lustful.

126

With the two women so inwardly turned, lunch was a somewhat silent affair. Silver clicked discreetly on china, as one course followed the last, the gurgle of wine being poured into the crystal goblets competed with the hum of insects outside in the garden. The three were grateful when the meal neared a close. Duval entered the room just as Pauline was placing her napkin back on the table.

"Oh, Colonel," she trilled. "So you are back from wherever you were. How charming. Will we have the pleasure of your company at dinner this evening?"

"It depends, Madame, on what the General needs me to do." He turned to Leclerc, at the head of the table, and clicked his boots together.

"General, I await your command."

"I wish to know how many workers are still in the cane fields at La Colline Verte," he said, "and how many house servants could be sent down for Madame's next soiree. The rebels seem in check at the present, so if you would designate one of your men to ride out and gain the necessary information for me."

"Shall I go myself?" inquired Duval. "Perhaps Madame Boucher would like to accompany me? She may have instructions for her major domo, which I could convey, of course. But perhaps Madame would like to ride out this afternoon..." he trailed off, not looking Odette in the eye.

"I would be delighted, Colonel," said Odette. "If Madame can spare me?" She turned to Pauline who was watching her through narrowed eyes.

"But of course," she said graciously. "Perhaps it is time for Odette to try out some of the activities I recommended this morning to assuage the pain of her recent loss. Yes, Madame?" she turned to Odette.

"As Madame wishes." Odette started intently at the napkin in her lap.

"Then it is so. As for me, I feel fatigue coming on after the over large meal. I will retire to my chamber for a rest. Leclerc, perhaps you would care to join me?"

Her husband immediately rose, offered his arm, and led Pauline up the stairs again and into their chamber.

'Another romp in the bed,' thought Odette. Truly her mistress was insatiable!

"Let me change into my riding attire," she said to Duval. "Would you care for some wine? Something to eat?"

"Perhaps a glass of wine while I wait for you," said Duval. "Please take your time." He rose from the table and bowed her out of the room.

Odette and Duval rode in companionable silence most of the way out to the plantation, threading their way through the streets of the town until they reached the foothills that led up to the higher elevation of the plateaus where the cane fields stretched seemingly for miles. After their talk in the salon the previous evening they were much more at ease with each other. A trip to La Colline Verte would, no doubt, cement their relationship; anything was possible with two young people both of whom were now free.

At the house Jacques hastened down the steps to greet them, calling to one of the yard boys to take the horses away to the stables and tend to them.

"I have prepared two rooms upstairs for you," he told them. "I thought you might wish to rest after the hot ride up here. I can have a bath prepared or wine taken to your rooms, just instruct me in your wishes."

Odette gazed fondly on this man who was her father. Shock though it had been to learn the truth, she was pleased that at least one of her parents was still alive, and happy to give her every possible assistance. Now was not the time to let Duval in on the secret, but if their relationship progressed as she hoped it would, she would tell him then.

"A bath would be wonderful after the hot ride," she said. "Thank you for thinking of it."

"I will have the water taken up." He disappeared toward the back of the house and the detached kitchen to give the necessary orders.

Odette mounted the stairs, Duval at her side. They found two open doors on the upstairs bedroom corridor: the one she had shared with Boucher and the adjacent one, in readiness for Duval. How tactful of Jacques to let them have the option of a room which had never been a nuptial chamber! Between the two rooms was a smaller one, used previously for a dressing room, and here was installed the tub for Odette's bath.

Duval left her at her own door, with a light kiss on her hand, and went the few yards down the hall to his own chamber.

Odette lay her hat, gloves and riding crop down on the dressing table, then sat on the stool and examined her face in the mirror. Instead of the wretched, miserable visage she had seen here only days before, she now viewed the glowing, happy face of a woman in love. The transformation was almost shocking. She put her hands up to her pink cheeks and held herself still for a few moments, savoring the feeling of anticipation of what she was sure was to come.

Sounds in the next room indicated that the servants were filling up the tub with buckets of water which had been standing in readiness on the stove. She went next door to supervise. Three young black maids, who were giggling over their task, stopped the minute they saw Odette in the doorway.

"Please don't stop on my account," she said. "And when you are through, you may go. I do not need any help in taking my bath."

They completed their task and rushed out the door. Odette heard their bare feet slapping on the treads of the staircase.

She stood by the tub expectantly. Immediately the door to Duval's room opened and he entered the room, crossing over to Odette and taking her in his arms. He had removed his heavy riding jacket and his boots and was dressed only in a flowing linen shirt with silk stockings thrust up under his canary britches.

"My love!" he exclaimed. "We are at last alone and together. It hardly seems possible."

"But it is true," she murmured into his neck, then quietly added, "I am ready."

No further words needed to be spoken; he understood her completely.

He led her over to a low stool and seated her, dropping to his knees before her, worshipping her beauty and her complete trust in him.

Slowly and gently he removed one small boot, then the other, putting them neatly by the side of the stool, then reached up under her riding skirt to find her garters, which he unfastened with practiced ease. He drew the silk stockings down and over her ankles and feet, caressing each one as he did so.

A tingle started up between Odette's legs, causing her to gasp in pleasure as Duval continued.

He took up the bath sponge and commenced washing her feet, carefully soaping each toe, the high instep, the ankle. He then lifted a new sponge which he wrung out in the warm bath water, and rinsed over what he has just washed. Gently he took each toe in turn into his mouth, sucking it while he massaged the delicate skin of her thigh, causing Odette to arch her back and begin emitting soft moans.

"Am I hurting you, my love?" he asked. "Is there anything I am doing that does not give you pleasure? Tell me if you want me to stop, now or at any other time, and I will immediately do so."

"No," she managed to gasp. "Do not stop." She gave herself over to the truly sensual pleasure of his caresses.

Her feet washed and dried, Duval rose to his knees and once again clasped Odette in his arms. He was so much taller and broader than she that his caress engulfed her, making her fell small and frail against his true manliness.

She tipped up her head, the better to receive his kisses. He began by a gentle pressure of his lips against her temple, moving to behind her ear, then his tongue flicked once, twice, gently into the delicate inside of her ear. Finally, his lips moved onto hers, sucking gently until she returned the pressure and opened her mouth, the better to receive his tongue.

All this while the pressure build up in the secret place between Odette's legs, causing her to let forth more intense moans of pleasure. She held tight to Duval's head, never wanting to let go.

A small chuckle escaped his lips as he put his hands to the small buttons of her blouse, unfastening each one with exactitude, finally drawing the garment over her shoulders and down off her back. She sat before him, dressed only in her camisole and riding skirt, under which were voluminous petticoats and the skimpiest of silk knickers.

He unfastened the skirt and drew it and the petticoats over her rounded hips, lifting her up for a moment to disengage her from the folds. His hands reached up to her shoulders, pushing down the straps of the camisole, allowing her perfect breasts to bob free, removing the garment as he went. He bent his head over her, taking first one nipple, then the other, into his warm, moist mouth, sucking gently until the darker aureoles puckered and hardened.

Swiftly he pulled the satin ribbon that held up the knickers, pushing them down past the black bush of her pubis, exposing all of her to his adoring gaze.

He stood now, picking her up like a feather and carrying her the few feet to the tub, where he deposited her into the welcoming warmth of the water. She sank back, luxuriating in the sloshing liquid, hoping this lesson in the art of love would never end.

Duval knelt now beside the tub, taking up again one of the sponges and commencing to wash her, starting with her neck, then down over her lovely breasts, down past her naval, down to the nether regions which had never, until then, known any pleasure from a man's touch. The sponge disappeared between her legs, rubbing over the tender vulva, causing yet further spasms of desire.

Odette felt as if she was on fire, and would soon burn up if her carnal urge was not soon satisfied. She tried to convey this to Duval by grabbing the hand that held the sponge, pressing it against her most sensitive parts, urging him on in his ministrations.

"Not so fast," he intoned, moving the sponge down her trembling thighs, over her knees, down to the small feet which he had so recently washed. "Not here." He rose up to his full height and, sopping wet though she was, lifted her from the now tepid water and strode through the door to his chamber.

Odette breathed a small sigh of relief. They would not now be making love in the chamber she had shared with her husband. Jacques had thought of everything by giving Duval the chamber that opened from the bath room, a place she had never entered before. It would be a wonderful new beginning for their love.

Duval laid Odette down on the bed, where a large linen sheet had been laid over the bedding. It was if Jacques had known he would dry her here after the bath, lay down the body he was almost mad to possess.

Odette reached up for him, fully clothed though he was. "Come to me, my love, my darling," she breathed. "Make me yours forever."

Duval let out a small chuckle. "My clothes would be an impediment of what you desire, Madame," he said almost jokingly. "Shall you help me, or shall I disrobe myself?"

"Oh, let me help you," she cried. "As you helped me."

Obligingly, Duval presented himself before her, waiting to see what she would do.

With no knowledge of the workings of men's clothes, Odette sat up, prepared to give it her all.

The shirt soon came off, over his head, exposing the manly chest whreon a small mat of hair sprouted between far apart nipples. Tentatively she reached up and stroked up these nipples, causing them to harden and a groan to escape from Duval's lips.

"So you enjoy this, too?" she asked coquettishly. Somehow, with this man before her she was able to summon all kinds of feminine wiles of which she had no knowledge. What she was doing, for the first time, seemed so natural as to make it all easy.

132

"Oh, yes, I enjoy this too," he told her, letting his hand trail over her breast even as she caressed him.

"Now the britches. Where do they fasten?"

He indicated a see of buttons each side of the front flap. "Try there, Madame."

Happily, she complied. The britches fell down of their own accord, leaving nothing underneath.

"You wear no undergarment?" she asked in mock surprise.

"Not needed, Madame. Only a hindrance."

"I see," she said playfully. "Then you are ready for any lady to disrobe you thus?"

"Only you." He gazed down on her adorable face.

His penis, greatly engorged with blood, stood at attention, bobbing between them.

She gasped in sheer pleasure at its size and heft. Is this the pleasure giver that will enter me with such sweet abandon and make me writhe in joy?" she asked.

"Let us certainly hope so."

"It is magnificent," she told him, inwardly comparing it to her own husband's much shorter and insignificant shaft.

"It would be best," he told her, "if we could remove my stockings and the britches completely. At present they would only serve to hamper me."

Looking at his britches hanging around his ankles, forestalling much movement, they both laughed.

"Allow me." He sat on the bed next to her, stripped off the stockings then drew the offending britches over his feet where they dropped to the floor. He was now as naked as she, a spectacular specimen of manhood from his well turned calves to the top of his curly head.

Odette admired her lover for a single moment before he dropped again to his knees by the bed, taking each foot on one of his hands and gently drawing her toward the edge, so that she was spread-eagled before him.

With the tiniest of kisses, caresses and licks from his warm red tongue he commenced his assault of her, first her feet and ankles, then up her calves, finally to her thighs which were twitching in anticipation of his finally entering her sopping wet vagina. He buried his nose in the thatch of her bush, parting it and exposing the beauty of her vulva. Tongue and fingers probed, explored, caressed, bringing forth ever more intense moans from Odette. She was panting now, her head thrashing on the pillow. The only words she could utter were 'no' and 'please', repeated at an ever and ever higher pitch.

Duval rubbed the small nubbin of her clitoris with his thumb, gently inserting two fingers, which he had moistened in his own mouth, into her vagina. Under him, her body melted with desire, her hips involuntarily dancing the movement of fucking. She was ready.

He slid himself upward, moving her small weight to the middle of the bed, swinging up her legs. She opened them to him, reaching out her arms to take him in her embrace as he so gently, so carefully, slid the length and breadth of his huge hard on past the parted labia, into the heaven and warmth of her slippery vagina.

Her mouth opened in an 'oh', but it was enough.

Together they rode the waves of desire, in perfect harmony, perfectly fused. It was as if his penis had been made to fit perfectly into her vagina, their rhythms matched exactly somewhere back at the beginning of time.

Wave after wave of pleasure, so intense it was almost like pain, washed over Odette. Higher and higher, more and more intense it rose, until she was screaming like an animal into the ear of her lover. All at once it was as if a plethora of shooting starts burst inside her, carrying her up into the heavens, pounding and streaming through her, until, for an instant, she actually lost consciousness, then drifted back down to the welcoming earth, where her lover's shout of triumph rang in her ear and they fell together back to reality.

Neither one felt the need to speak, clasped as they were in each other's arms. The sexual experience had been so intense, so perfect, as to defy description. It was enough that they were together, that they had finally consummated their perfect love.

Odette gazed deeply into her lover's eyes, and he into hers, until both drifted off in to the heavenly slumber only experienced by two who had experienced perfect sexual love.

Chapter Seven

Retreat

As the hot summer of 1803 wore on, more and more of the native troops that had come over to the French side only months before began to desert and return to the mountains where the rebels still held sway. They were so firmly entrenched, and the terrain was so rough, Leclerc's army had no hope of dislodging them. More and more of the French soldiers continued to die, making for a dire situation for their commander. His only hope of holding the island was through military force, which prospect grew dimmer and dimmer with each passing day.

Against this gloom and doom the romance between Odette and Duval continued to grow and bloom. They spent every free moment they had together, under the indulgent eye of Pauline Leclerc, who cheered the lovers on and found numerous ways to throw them together...and leave them alone.

July waned and August came, with even more oppressive heat and more deaths among the French troops. Any possible hope of a diplomatic solution to the island's problems was gone now, leaving only the few remaining French troops to stave off a total massacre of the whites who were still in residence in the towns and the scattered plantations. The additional troops requested by Leclerc never arrived and he feared all his former successes would come to naught and the island would again be overrun by the hoards of black rebels, which would spell the end of any French presence in San Domingue...forever. It was truly a black time for the Governor, though Pauline continued to maintain her equilibrium, and even kept on with her soirees and parties.

"It is necessary to keep our spirits up," she would say, sending for the musicians to practice new songs and the chefs to invent new dishes to tempt her guests.

In September, word came to the Governor that a huge insurrection was planned by the rebel troops for the 16th. He gathered up the few remaining soldiers who were well enough to fight, and sent word throughout Le Cap for ordinary citizens to arm themselves and prepare to defend their town and the island against the coming onslaught. He also ordered Pauline to pack up only what was absolutely necessary and prepare to abandon the Residence for the relative safety on one of the ships of the fleet still anchored in the town's harbor.

Pauline rose to her true strength during this time, declaring that, as a sister of Napoleon she was not afraid to die, and would gladly give her life for France. Noble sentiments which, fortunately, were not carried out.

The sixteenth came. From the relative safety of the Governor's Residence, Pauline and Odette, with Duval in attendance as Captain of the Guard, watched from an upstairs balcony as the troops streamed out of the center to do battle with the rebels advancing from the hills. All around the town fires blazed, lit by the black troops. Odette prayed that La Colline Verte had not been consumed and hoped that Jacques and the other servants were not being butchered at this very moment. She need not have worried. News of her true parentage had spread via gossip of the house servants to all corners of the island, and Odette was now considered to be 'one of them' as opposed to a French citizen, attempting to wrest the island from its true natives.

All morning the battle raged around the outskirts of the town; various dispatches sent to Duval were conflicting: the French army was subduing the native troops; the native troops were taking over. All was in chaos and no one knew the truth of how the fight was going.

Duval had been given instructions that, were the black troops to storm the town, he was to immediately evacuate his wife and child, Odette and any French servants to the harbor and onto the ships. An order came at noon, and Duval went into action.

"Madame," he turned to address Pauline. "Your husband has commanded that you proceed at once to the harbor and take ship, you and the child and Madame Boucher. If you hesitate or refuse, then I am to carry you bodily there."

"Oh, I am perfectly safe here," Pauline replied. "I have no intention of fleeing. I, the sister of Napoleon!" Her eyes snapped and twin circles of red suffused her cheeks. "I am not afraid!"

Fearing just this reaction, Duval motioned to Odette. "Madame, prepare the Governor's lady for departure. And make sure the child and his nurse are ready as well. We leave immediately." He summoned four of the strongest servants at his disposal, and indicated they were to pick up the divan on which Pauline was lounging. They lifted it as if it were a feather, with her still lounging, and carried it out through the house and onto the wide steps that led down to the harbor.

Dermide, hand in hand with his nurse, followed closely behind. Duval, escorting Odette brought up the rear of the little procession while the household guard fell in behind.

From houses along the way women and children streamed, swelling the march, requesting too that they be taken on board the ships, to avoid capture and death at the hands of the rebels. All in all it was a raggle taggle bunch, from Pauline, queenly on her divan, though skimpily dressed in only a morning peignoir, which constantly fell open and was clutched coquettishly to her perfect breasts. The town woman were dressed in everything from nightclothes to formal day dresses of stiff material which were set off by giant hats with plumes, ribbons and flowers. This motley group progressed slowly down toward the harbor, only to be halted half way there by a young French soldier, who pulled up on a lathered horse and handed yet another dispatch to Duval.

He broke the seal and scrutinized the document, recognizing it for a bone fide order from his general.

"Citizens of Le Cap," he shouted at the top of his lungs, the better to be heard by the group of chattering women, "the town is saved! The rebels are beaten back. Thanks be to God. You may all safely return to your homes." He clasped Odette in his arms, never wanting to let her go.

"My darling, you are safe. I could not have borne the sorrow of losing you." He buried his face in her hair.

"I always had faith you would bring us through safely," she murmured into his ear. "But I must attend to Madame." Reluctantly she turned her attention to Pauline who was waving joyously to the crowd.

"We are saved!" she exclaimed. "My husband has once again been victorious. Do come to the Residence this evening; we will have a party to celebrate the victory and to cheer my husband. Until then..." She was borne away up again toward the Residence, smiling and bowing to all.

Odette and Duval settled Pauline in her suite upon arrival back at the residence. Both were experiencing a surfeit of nerves from the recent ordeal. It was a lucky outcome to the shelling of the town, which could just as easily have gone in favor of the rebels.

Duval grabbed Odette by the wrist, hurrying her away from Pauline's apartments, breathing so hard his face was red up to the roots of his hair. Without ceremony he pulled her into an alcove partly hidden by a screen where he backed her up to a wall.

She grasped him around the neck, holding him with all her strength, straining against the long, hot body, with a massive erection straining the front of his trousers.

"My darling!" he exclaimed, 'If I had lost you....'

"My beloved. You were magnificent." She fumbled for the buttons on his trousers at the same moment he reached up under her skirts, ripping her pantaloons savagely off her body, tearing the thin material to shreds. Without any preliminaries, he lifted her atop his rampant penis, and shoved it fully into her dripping vagina. It took only a few strokes for both of them to gasp in ecstasy and climax together in one violent spurt of suppressed energy, moaning and straining one against the other. In a few seconds, all was over. Duval placed her again on the ground with all the care of standing a fragile china statuette atop a mantelpiece, letting her dress fall around her ankles. He dropped to his knees in front of Odette, taking a fold of her hem into his hand and bringing it, almost reverently, up to his lips.

"Forgive me, my darling, my dearest," he murmured. "It was unthinkable what I just did, but I was so desperate to prove we are both alive and safe I forgot myself for a moment. It will never happen again." He kept his head bowed, not sure what her reaction would be.

"There is nothing to forgive," she told him. "I felt exactly the same. It was a vindication of our life force, glorifying the fact we had escaped a terrible end. I love you all the more for it." She drew him up so he was once again standing, and leaned up on tiptoe to fuse his lips with hers in a long and lingering kiss.

"And now we are safe," she said with a little trill. "Let us retire to our chamber. I am sure we could use some rest and refreshment after our ordeal." Gaily she took his hand and led him, unprotesting, down the corridor to their chamber where they more slowly demonstrated their love for each other on the soft, wide bed.

Odette secretly hoped that a child might have been conceived in that alcove, one who would become a great soldier like his father.

A couple of days after the triumph of the Battle of Le Cap, Duval again rode out to La Colline Verte, this time alone. He was sent to assess the damage to the plantation and report back to both Leclerc and Odette. It was with a sense of foreboding he turned in at the gates and cantered up the drive toward the plantation house. What would he find? A burned and ruined shell? Broken window and all the flowers in the gardens trampled beneath the feet of men and horses?

Instead, to his astonishment, when he gained the forecourt the house looked just the same, slumbering in the mid morning sunlight. The verandah was just as welcoming; the vines still swirled and twirled around the posts holding up the broad roof, the windows sparkled just as brilliantly, and, on the steps, Jacques was waiting to greet him.

Amazed, Duval dismounted and threw his reins to a waiting stable boy.

"Good morning, Colonel," Jacques intoned.

"Good morning, Jacques," replied Duval. "Will you be so kind as to wait on me in the dining room?"

"Certainly, sir. Would you care for refreshments? Perhaps some wine?"

"Yes, please." His boots rang heavily across the boards of the verandah and he entered the wide front hall, relatively cool at this hour of the morning. He went down the hall and pushed open the double doors of the dining room. All was as it should be. The silver candelabra on the table, the serving pieces on the sideboard, gleamed brightly in the shafts of sunlight coming through the long French windows and all were intact. The long length of the polished mahogany table was mirror like in its perfection and all the chairs were lined up precisely in their places, eight to each side and one armchair at each end.

Duval took up his place at the foot of the table. Jacques entered a moment later with a tall green bottle, a glass and a small plate of cheeses and meats, which he lay down with great ceremony before Duval.

"Thank you, Jacques. Please sit down with me...oh, and fetch another glass for yourself. I know who you are now, Madame Odette has told me, and I honor you for your place in her life."

"I thank you, sir," the Major Domo replied, "but I have been a servant all my life and would be uncomfortable sitting in your presence and taking wine with you. It is enough that my daughter recognizes me for what I am, for which I am eternally thankful." He stood a respectful distance away from the table, hands folded in front of him.

"Very well," said Duval. "I have no wish to make you uncomfortable in any way. I am here this morning to find out why this plantation was spared, when so many in the surrounding area are no more than ashes now."

Jacques took a moment to reply. "I will tell you the truth, sir, though it may heap trouble on my head and even mean imprisonment for me. For many years prior to the arrival of M. Le General, this house was used by Christophe and his officers as a headquarters in this part of the island. The great Toussaint himself visited here on many occasions and even spent the night in the rooms that are now used by General Leclerc and his wife. This is one reason why the house and the plantation were in such good shape when Mme. Odette returned home after so long an absence. I had to keep things up for their sake, as well as for the sake of the rightful owner. The officers and men cleared out as soon as your fleet was sighted on the other end of the island, and all evidence of their stay here was eradicated by me. That is why the plantation was spared, and will be forevermore, especially now Mme. Odette has acknowledged me as her father."

This astonishing speech left Duval speechless for a few moments. Finally he collected his thoughts together enough to reply. "Then you mean," he said slowly. "That La Colline Verte will forever be a safe place for Odette and all who are connected with her? Through her and the leaders of the rebellion, whichever way the final outcome goes."

Jacques bowed low. "Exactly, Monsieur," he said.

Duval digested this reply in silence, though a myriad of new ideas collected in his head.

"And what do you think the outcome of this war for the freedom of San Domingue will be?" he asked.

"I hesitate to say," replied Jacques. "But the people of San Dominquez fight for their homeland, the French, for a land that is far away and have a real connection to this island. Except for the profit it can bring, of course. I would therefore say that the uprising that began thirty years ago will at length be over and the island will belong to us." He bowed his head before the would-be conqueror.

142

"Then so be it," exclaimed Duval. "Thank you for your information and for your candor. You will have no reason to regret either." He rose from the table, his wine untouched. "I must get back to town with my report. Continue in the good work here, Jacques." He touched his heels together in recognition of the great gifts bestowed by the Major Domo, and took his departure.

Jacques stood on the steps of the verandah for a long time after the cloud of dust caused by the departing soldiers and their Colonel had fallen back to the red clay of the long driveway.

Back at the Governor's Residence at Le Cap, Duval was uncertain about whom he should report to first. Discovering that Leclerc was out inspecting the troops and ascertaining what damage had been done to the town, he decided to see Odette first. Fortunately, he found her alone in the small salon, stitching on her endless embroidery.

"My darling," he said, throwing himself down on one of the slender-legged chairs beside her. "I have the best of news. The plantation was spared entirely by the rebel troops. All is as it was before we left a few days ago. "Your Jacques..." he corrected himself, "your father is amazing. He told me that the house had been used by some of the officers of this uprising for many years past, and for that reason was spared in this recent skirmish and will be spared for all time. Do you know what that means?"

"Yes," said Odette calmly, "it means I never have to return to France, that I can remain here for all my life."

"Is that what you want?"

"Yes," said Odette steadily. "I know now I am a part of this island, as was my mother, and, with my mixed blood will always be safe here. I and any who choose to remain with me. I have no relatives alive in France. Either natural death or the guillotine got them all. " She did not say any of this archly, but with true sincerity. She looked straight into Duval's eyes.

"And would I be one whom you would choose to have stay with you?" he asked. "Forever?"

"You, only you," she breathed.

Duval dropped to one knee before her. "Then will you do me the honor of becoming my wife? I will love and cherish you forever and will ensure our children love this place of your birth as much as I am coming to love it."

It will give me the greatest pleasure to become your wife," said Odette, giving Duval her hand.

He grasped it with delight and covered it with ardent kisses.

"My true love. I will strive forever to be worthy of you."

Neither had noticed, so enraptured were they with each other, but the door had opened and Pauline had witnessed most of the tender scene.

"Congratulations are certainly in order," she trilled. "Tiens, a marriage to plan. It is the least I can do for you two and it will detract our thoughts from the situation going on all around you. Shall you marry here or go back to France?"

Without thinking or consulting each other, they both spoke at once.

"Here, of course, Madame," from Odette.

"On San Domingue," said Duval, "as we plan on making this island our home.

"Then so shall it be," declared Pauline. "I will so inform Leclerc the moment I see him. "And now, I think, some champagne." She crossed the room and rang the bell cord to order the wine. "Tonight we will have a dual celebration: the betrothal and the citizens coming here to offer their congratulations to Leclerc. It will be a grand event, let me tell you. Now I must go consult with the cooks, musicians and household staff. No, Madame," she said to Odette. "Do not rise. This is one party I will oversee all by myself. I am going to have to learn to live without you soon enough, when the General and I return to France." She turned and floated out of the room, humming a little tune. Truly two things made Pauline ecstatic: sex and parties. Today promised some of each.

Chapter Eight

Hail and Farewell

The wedding was set for October 15, by which time, it was hoped, the weather would be somewhat cooler. In any case, the Leclercs were anxious to return to France. The General realized that the peace on the island was fragile at best; all his hopes and plans for a glorious win for France were coming to naught and he was hopeful that Napoleon would send someone out to relieve him, soon.

Pauline was agog with plans for what would be her most lavish and extravagant party: the nuptials of her beloved lady in waiting and Leclerc's Colonel Duval, who would remain with the Creole beauty when the rest of the French expedition sailed for home...whenever that might be. In the meantime, it was wonderful to have this diversion.

She ransacked the stores she had brought out from France to make the Duvals life more comfortable, turning up bales of dress fabric and upholstery, shawls and hats and shoes and trim to complete the most extensive of trousseaus for the bride. She planned to leave Odette with all the silver, glass and china she had brought out for her own use. No need to pack it up and haul it back to France when so much more of the same would be available to her once she was back in Paris. It was a bountiful gesture to Odette, but one Pauline was happy to make. When did one have the sole authority to plan a wedding, moreover a wedding on a God-forsaken tropical island? It would be the crowning achievement of her social life to give Odette the same sort of wedding she might have enjoyed were she back home in France.

To this end Pauline called in all the best dressmakers, curtain makers, upholsterers and furniture makers, to produce the goods to render the plantation house at La Colline Verte as much like a French chateau as possible. With almost unlimited help and funds at hand, it proved simpler than she originally thought, and by the second week of September, all was in readiness.

Because the plantation had been so thoroughly refurbished, and because Odette and Duval would be making their home there, she planned the event to take place at La Colline Verte, not at the Governor's Residence in town. Besides, the plantation house, built eighty years before, had a charm and patina that did not exist in the newly constructed official residence, which was raw and sloppily erected. La Colline Verte would provide a far more suitable background for the wedding itself, which would take place in the small chapel, attended only by a few of the guests. The reception, which would be all over the ground floor of the house, incorporating the wide veranda that ran around three sides, would accommodate as many guests as Pauline – and Odette – wanted. The list was expanded daily, until at least three hundred were bidden to the grand dinner, followed by dancing, that would follow the wedding itself.

While the two women planned and organized and drove everyone crazy, Leclerc and Duval spent time riding around the environs of Le Cap and up into the foothills, making sure no more large insurrections were at hand. They wanted nothing to interfere with the celebration surrounding the wedding, nor did Leclerc know how much more time he and Pauline had on the island. Letters back and forth to France could take up to three months... or more. Leclerc had no idea if the next boat out from France would carry his replacement, or a letter from Napoleon telling him who that replacement would be and when he would arrive. While that matter was certainly up in the air, it seemed prudent to get the wedding accomplished and let the newly married Duvals establish themselves on the plantation.

During that hurried, busy month, the engaged couple pledged to refrain from any sexual congress, the sweeter to make their wedding night. While it was torture, at times, to stay away from each other, they prevailed and when the morning of October 15 dawned bright and clear, with a tiny breeze from the harbor stirring up brief wafts of cooler air, they were more than ready to consummate their love for each other.

Odette woke to the sound of the cocks crowing, and stretched languidly in the single bed in which she had been sleeping for the past four weeks. She had moved to another wing of the house, having no desire to spend another night in the bed or the room which she had shared with her husband. When she and Duval came together this very night, they would be in yet a different part of the large house, one which had been occupied by neither of them before. In this way would they begin their married life on new terms and in a new place.

She got up, used the chamber pot and returned to bed, where she fell into a dreamless slumber until a soft tap on her door heralded the arrival of her morning coffee.

"Come in," she called and a small black girl entered, tray carefully balanced in her hands.

"Mornin' Mistress,"the girl said softly. "Felicitations on you' weddin' day."

"Why, thank you," said Odette. "What a lovely start to what I hope will be a lovely day.

"Yessum, Mistress." The girl placed the tray carefully across Odette's knees and withdrew soundlessly.

On the tray, alongside the silver pot and the china plate holding a croissant and a generous pat of butter was a single, perfect rose bud. She picked it up and smelled the fragrance. It even held a few drops of early morning dew. A card lay under it.

'May this be symbol of my love for you, which will only blossom and grow as we make our way forward in life, forever joined as one.' A single initial followed. Odette caught up the card and pressed it to her lips, then fell to with gusto and consumed her simple breakfast, reflecting that she was always hungry these days, though sometimes the early morning food gave her nausea. He breasts, too, had become somewhat swollen and tender, both signs to her that that long ago mating had, indeed, produced a child, or at least the beginning of one. She hugged herself happily. She, too would have a 'premature' baby, just like her mother, though this one would be borne in wedlock, unlike herself. She would save the news to tell Duval when they would be together – and alone – in the new matrimonial chamber, in the large matrimonial bed which had been fashioned by the best cabinet maker on the island, the mattress stuffed with pounds and pounds of Pauline's feathers, brought over for just such an event. She rose and crossed over to the long windows giving out on the veranda, the better to examine this beautiful day which would be her wedding day. All shone and sparkled, the glass in the windows, the furniture all around the house, the plethora of silver and glass that was even now being laid out on long tables for the later pleasure of the wedding guests. Pauline had overlooked nothing; it promised to be a perfect day. Odette executed a tiny twirl, then rang for her Marie Claire to help her dress, making sure Pauline had completed her own toilette and had no further need of the woman.

All morning and long after lunch the servants hustled and bustled around the house and grounds, setting up chairs, sweeping the already perfectly swept driveway, trimming the tiny chapel with boughs of fragrant white roses and yellow mimosa. Large vases burst with flowers throughout the house, in hues complimenting the colors Pauline had selected for the decoration of the rooms: yellows, whites, sky blues. The azure sky held a few puffy clouds, but no sign of rain, though a cloudburst could happen at any time. Everyone hoped if this did not occur it would at least hold off until after the wedding itself, but as it never materialized, all could breathe a sigh of relief.

148

At two in the afternoon, Pauline swept in to Odette's room, to help dress the bride. She was costumed in lime green satin, with a higher neckline than usual, for on this one day she had no wish to outshine the bride. Her hair was in an elaborate coiffure of ringlets and puffs, surmounted by a diamond aigrette and white ostrich feathers, which nodded under the fan, as always manned by a small boy in the corner of the room, to whom no one paid the least attention.

Odette had already bathed, and was clad only in a light peignoir, with no undergarments under it. These, of the slightest wisp of chiffon, hand embroidered and embellished with lace, lay ready over the back of a chair. Pauline herself helped Odette into these lovely items, smoothing the material over her breasts, tucking down a bit of the lace so it would not peep over the top of the wedding gown.

This was fashioned of the sheerest cotton lawn, pale rose in color, bound tightly under the now fuller breasts, which strained a bit at the material.

"Tiens," muttered Pauline, "you seem to have gained weight since the last fitting...." She broke off her reverie. "But of course, you are with child. How charming. How fitting! Since you have decided to remain here you are already beginning a dynasty that will keep the family name going for at least a generation to come. Congratulations, my dear." She bent down and kissed Odette, first on one cheek, then the other.

"Please let me be the one to tell Duval," Odette pleaded. "I was saving the news for this night."

"But of course," agreed Pauline, "it is your news and not for me to share. I sometimes wonder, with all the trying I do with Charles, we do not have more children than Dermide. A little sister or brother would be nice for him, but I do not seem to be able to conceive again. Perhaps when we return to France and things calm down somewhat..." she broke off. "But what a conversation for you on this very day! Now let me see how we can contain these lovely breasts within your bodice. It would not do for them to pop out just as the priest is pronouncing you man and wife!" She gave a gay trill and fussed with the material of the bodice, pulling it up slightly where it once again gave way to the rounded mounds rising from its folds.

Marie Claire stood in the background, making approving noises as Pauline continued with her dressing of the bride, placing a crown of roses on her flowing hair, unbound for this one last day when she was to appear to be – once again – a virgin bride and handing her a bouquet of matching flowers, bound with long satin ribbons in white and pale rose to match the gown. At length she stepped back to view her handiwork.

"You may now view yourself in the mirror," she told Odette. "You are truly the picture of the beautiful, blushing bride."

Odette obediently turned to the long glass, in the corner of the room. She saw a lovely young creature, charmingly robed, eyes sparkling as she thought of the ceremony to come which would join her forever to the object of her love. Impulsively she turned to Pauline and gave her the gentlest of hugs, the better to muss neither of their costumes.

"Ah, Madame," she exclaimed, 'you have surely been my friend for all these months, my friend and my mentor. I can never repay you for all your kindnesses."

"But it will all be worth if only you are happy."

"Then it has indeed been worth it," Odette told her. "For never was a bride happier than I."

Someone knocked on the door. It was Leclerc, who was to escort the bride to the chapel.

They proceeded together down the wide staircase. In the front hall all the house servants were lined up, all starched and smiling. They called greetings and good luck to the bride as she crossed the porch, her arm in Leclerc's, from where they walked the short distance to the family chapel, which was located at the end of an allee of palms and tropical flowers, growing in profusion and vivid colors. Pauline's native musicians preceded the couple, serenading them on their way.

The service, shortened from its usual hour duration owing to the heat, went without a hitch and at three thirty precisely the priest intoned the words to conclude the ceremony:

"I now pronounce you man and wife. May you so live together in this life that in the life to come you may find peace everlasting."

Duval bent to kiss his radiant bride, the offered her his arm for the trip back down the aisle. All around them rose murmurs of approbation, while outside, on the chapel steps, Duval's officers had raised their swords, making an arch of gleaming steel for the bridal couple to walk under.

The afternoon and early evening passed in a haze for Odette, as she ate and drank and danced and exchanged pleasantries with so many of the wedding guests, all of whom had come to wish her and Duval well. Finally, it was time for the couple to withdraw, leaving their guests to continue with the party without the bridal pair. They mounted the stairs to the upper veranda and took up a stance over the main door, with all the guests gathered underneath. Odette took her bouquet, gave it one last caress and tossed it over the balcony rail, to be caught by one of the single female guests, all of whom were hoping to be the lucky young woman to grasp the roses. There were cries all around, with one standing out from the rest: the girl who caught the flowers. Her friends gathered around, congratulating her, taking the focus off Odette and Duval who slipped back through the window and tiptoed down the long corridor to the back of the house and their bridal chamber. Waiting were their maid and valet, who ushered them behind matching screens in opposite corners of the room, disrobing them and redressing them in nightshirt and lacy peignoir. Their task completed, they bowed and curtsied and let themselves out.

They also dismissed the small boy in the corner who endlessly plied his string attached to the overhead fan. This was one night when they wished to be totally alone. He padded across the floor, closing the door softly behind him.

Bride and groom turned to each other almost in wonderment.

"It is real," breathed Odette. "We are truly husband and wife." She leaned into his embrace.

"Indeed it is real," countered Duval. "Forever and ever."

A small shiver went down Odette's spine. It was supposed to be Boucher and Odette for all time, but fate had removed him from her life. She breathed a sigh of relief. Sometimes impossible situations resolved themselves. She gave herself a little shake. Boucher was gone. In his place stood this perfect man, whom she loved to the deepest depths of her soul.

He knelt at her feet for a moment, catching the hem of her robe and bringing it to his lips. "I adore, worship, cherish only you," he said humbly. "Now and forever."

She reached down for his curly head, running her fingers through his hair. She stretched her hands out to him, lifting him from his lowly position and led him over to the wide expanse of the bridal bed. This bed, a present from Pauline, was elaborately hung and draped with curtains embroidered with all the flowers of the island. Native seamstresses had worked morning, noon and night to finish the embroidery in time for the wedding night. It was a labor of much love and dedication, from the women on the plantation.

Together, Duval and Odette sank onto the softness of the down mattress, then both gave a yelp. Stuck here and there with tiny pricks, they stared in confusion at each other. Odette stood up and threw back the covers, exposing a tangle of scores and scores of white roses, strewn over the undersheet.

"Roses!" She exclaimed. "Roses for a soldier's bed!"

"It was well meant," said Duval, ruefully rubbing his backside through his linen nightshirt. "Even though the thought certainly went awry."

They gently combed the offending flowers from the sheets, placing them in a large heap on Odette's dressing table, another present from Pauline. It, too, had come from Versailles and was reputed to have belonged to the doomed Queen, Marie Antoinette. Set on spindly straight legs, in the classical style, it was embellished with magnificent plaques of Sevres porcelain, depicting all manner of plump cherubs floating in fleecy banks of white clouds.

Laughing, Odette sunk on the stool in front of the dressing table, and took up her hair brush.

"Here, let me." Duval relieved her of the brush and started to pull it gently through the long tresses, left free for the wedding. Tomorrow she would put it up into an elaborate coiffure as befitted a married woman. Tonight the lushness of the strands belonged only to him.

Rhythmically he plied the brush, so expertly that Odette felt like purring. A gentle wave of desire swept over her, starting from the prickling on her scalp down through her torso and into the inner regions that so longed for her husband. As if he felt her pleasure mounting, Duval dropped the brush, picked Odette up from the stool and carried her back to the bed, where he deposited her gently onto the soft mattress.

She kept her arms around his neck, as if she would never let go. Slowly, he lowered himself next to her, gazing deeply into her eyes all the while. They knew there was no haste in what was to come, that the consummation of their marriage would be one of the perfect events in their lives, to be remembered as long as they lived.

He reached out a hand and tenderly began to stroke her breast through the thin material of her peignoir. Odette groaned softly, thrusting out her chest. The stroking became firmer and she writhed, soundless now, pushing up against her husband, clutching his arms in her hands.

He reached inside the garment that covered Odette's charms, freeing the two globes of her breasts, which he bent over and covered with kisses. Taking one rosy nipple between his lips, then the other, he sucked and bit gently, eliciting a further moan from his wife.

"Touch me," he whispered in her ear. "Love me as I am loving you."

She reached inside the nightshirt, taking his nipples between thumb and forefinger, stroking and pinching, until his nipples hardened and stiffened and a groan forced itself from Duval's throat.

He drew open the sash of Odette's robe, exposing her in all her loveliness, and let his hand wander down from her breasts, over the still flat stomach, lingering on the black bush that sheltered all her sexual charms. She gave a sharp intake of breath, and arched her back, thrusting herself provocatively toward him. He needed no further invitation, but pressed an inquiring finger through the dark tangle, finding her vulva opened up to his ministrations. He gently stroked over the pulsing labia, lingering with each contact with her enlarged clitoris, moving gently inside her into her slippery, hot vagina, inserting then withdrawing one, then two fingers into its tight dark depths.

Instinctively, Odette reached down for his burgeoning erection, taking the stiffening penis into her warm, soft hand, squeezing and stroking alternately until Duval was moaning and writhing in sweet rhythm with that of his wife.

Their lovemaking seemed enough; there was no need for more elaborate foreplay, as each sought to deepen the moment between them. They were poised and ready to truly consummate their love and their legal union. Duval raised himself up above her, and, with no need to guide himself, slipped easily into the tender vessel so lovingly laid out before him. Together they forged the perfect union, fitting together as if they had been made only for each other, thrusting and withdrawing with mounting intensity until – looking again into each other's eyes, they exploded together into one earth shattering, perfect orgasm.

It was only then Odette told her new husband about the child that was within her. He clutched her fervently in his arms, and together they drifted off into a deep and peaceful slumber.

The following day all the wedding guests, including Pauline and Leclerc withdrew to the town below, leaving the bride and groom in seclusion for the honeymoon, which had been planned to last a month.

The couple made much of their time together, relieved on any duties or responsibilities. They rode out early each morning, often before the sun was fully up, discovering places in the plantation neither had ever seen before. Returning for breakfast, they often had time to mount to their room and, in changing from riding clothes to day attire, for a brief session of loving, always concluded by a mutually satisfying orgasm, before descending to the verandah for breakfast served by Jacques and one or two of the maids.

Duval often read while Odette sewed after the repast, often in companionable silence. They had no need to fill their time with idle chatter; so completely in accordance were they, each with the other.

After a light luncheon, they again retired to their quarters, to nap away the hottest part of the day, cool behind shutters and the generous roof of the upstairs verandah. These afternoon hours were often the time of their most intense lovemaking, as they sought new pleasures and new positions for the sexual act itself, heightening their already great passion for each other. Duval proved an experienced and a tender lover, leading Odette gently down the many paths of erotic bliss, ever mindful to pull back if she slowed the slightest sign of hesitation or fear. He had served with Napoleon in his Egyptian campaign, and had discovered many of the more exotic pleasures of the east, as demonstrated by the whores who followed the troops on their maneuvers.

Odette gradually came to realize that all Pauline had told her had come true; the more they made love the more wonderful it became, and the silly games they played in bed but heightened their pleasure. She came eagerly to these sessions, always desirous of pleasing her husband, but finding that, in doing so, she was pleasured too. And his eastern experiences only woke in her a sense of the erotic, surpassing even the many postures and much love play they attempted in the earlier days of wedded bliss.

On one such afternoon, six days after the wedding, the couple woke from their brief siesta, and turned toward each other, eager for their afternoon session of lovemaking to begin. They had begun to experiment with costumes, robbing themselves as desert sheiks and tribal maidens, as circus clowns and the ringmaster. This particular afternoon Odette was dressed in flowing harem trousers, her chest bound by the approximation of a belly dance's brassiere, in a tightly wrapped bronze scarf. Duval lounged on the bed in a brocade robe, brought back from Egypt, its stiff folds allowing the beginnings of an erection to peer out from under the satin facings. He had wound one of Odette's scarves, turban fashion, around his head and held a driving whip in his hand, which he flicked at her from time to time, making sure it never landed too near to do any harm.

Odette was switching her hips in her best imitation of a belly dancer, bare feet shuffling on the floor. She undulated closer and closer to the bed and finally fell atop her husband, who had a tremendous grin on his face and a matching hard on thrusting out from his robe. He reached for her crotch just as her hand closed on his penis.

A knock on the door brought them up short. Odette threw the sheet over her in an attempt to hide her provocative costume, while Duval pulled the folds of his robe over his pulsing manhood.

"Come in," he called.

Jacques entered sideways, doing his best not to look at the couple on the bed.

"Yes?" Said Duval somewhat icily.

"Pardon Monsieur. Madame. A message just came from Mme. Leclerc. The rider said it was urgent and was to be delivered to you immediately." He sidled up to the bed, keeping his eyes averted, and held out a silver salver on which was a sealed note. The seal bore the unmistakable cipher of Pauline and Odette snatched it up, breaking the seal. She unfolded the heavy parchment and read the brief note:

'Leclerc stricken with Siamese fever. Come at once.' There was no signature but Odette was familiar with the handwriting of her mistress.

"Oh, no!" She exclaimed. "Leclerc has the fever. She wants us with her at once." She rose from the bed, forgetting her attire. Somehow it no longer seemed to matter.

"May I give an answer to the courier, Madame?" Jacques had now turned his back on the couple and was standing by the door.

'Yes, Jacques," Odette told him. "Tell the courier that we will be on our way as soon as possible. And please have our horses saddled; it will be quicker to ride than take the carriage."

"Thank you Madame," replied the Major Domo who was also her father. He closed the door quietly behind him.

The trip into Le Cap was made swiftly. Upon arrival at the Residence, Odette hastened immediately to the quarters occupied by the Leclercs. She found Pauline prostrate on a divan, wringing her hands. Odette crossed the room and sank down beside her mistress, taking her hand.

"Ah, Madame, what dreadful news. We came immediately. I do hope the General is not too bad?"

"I do not know," wailed Pauline. "The doctors say it may not be the dreaded fever, just overwork and pressure. I pray it is the latter. He is so worn down with all the cares heaped on his shoulders I fear he does not have the strength to combat a serious illness." There were rivulets of recently shed tears on her cheeks, and her usually beautifully coiffed hair was in wild disarray.

"Let me tidy your person, Madame," offered Odette. "You would want the General to see you looking your best, the better to cheer him along at this trying time." She helped Pauline to her feet and led her gently to the adjacent dressing room, seating her at a low stool before her dressing table. "Fill the bath," she commanded to a hovering maid. "Quickly." The girl scurried off, to return shortly with several assistants, all carrying heavy copper cans of water and milk. She picked up the ornate silver brush and commenced brushing Pauline's hair in long, soothing strokes. Presently she helped her into the tub and, herself, took up the sponge, laving the rounded limbs and slathering tepid liquid over

Pauline's rounded breasts which bounced, pertly atop the liquid sloshing over the tub's edge.

At length Pauline calmed, leaning back in the tub gracefully. "Ah, Odette,' she said gratefully, "no one ever took care of me as you do. Alas, I am losing you when we sail for France."

"Will that be soon?" asked Pauline.

"Hopefully in the new year." Pauline told her. "My husband has heard that Napoleon is sending out the young General Rochambeau to replace him here."

"Rochambeau?" The name rang a bell.

"One of the heroes of the American Revolution," Pauline told her. "The name was familiar to me, too, so I asked Leclerc about him."

"Surely the General is too old for such duties which have been assigned to him?"

"I wondered, too," said Pauline. "This is not the old man; it is his son, who has followed in his father's footsteps."

"Of course." Odette's curiosity satisfied she took up a towel and helped Pauline out of the tub. Drying her tenderly, she took out fresh undergarments and Pauline's most flattering morning robe of thin sprigged lawn, ruched and tucked around the low square neckline, flowing gracefully in folds from under the bust. Once dressed, she again seated her mistress at her dressing table and commenced curling and braiding Pauline's hair, sweeping it up and pinning it around the crown. Stepping back, she admired her handiwork.

"Perfection," she exclaimed.

Pauline regarded herself critically in the mirror. "You have the magic touch," she told Odette gratefully. "Now I will go into Leclerc. Please do not accompany me; I do not want you to take the chance of infection. Especially not in your present condition." She patted her own stomach in acknowledgement of Odette's pregnancy, stood up and swept gracefully from the room.

Odette sank down on the just vacated stool, feeling somewhat weak and dizzy. No doubt the frenzied ride into town and the distress in which she found the Governor's lady. It was good to rest for a minute.

Initially, the doctor stuck to his original diagnosis: the General was simply overtired and overwrought. A few days in bed should make him well again. Rest and no worries. He should be restored to full health in very few days.

Five days later he seemed somewhat improved, and managed to show himself to the populace of the town from a balcony. He declared himself well enough to attend Pauline's soiree that evening, entering the ballroom between his wife and the doctor. He did not want to panic the population of Le Cap with his illness, which, in so many cases had led to death. Such an event might well terrify the whites still living on the island, and reverse any victories he may have won over the rebels.

His recovery, however, was short lived. At the soiree he went over to an open window to try to catch a breath of fresh air. The ballroom was alight with candles, redolent with the sickening sweet smell of too many flowers and too much perfume, and he was having a hard time catching his breath. At the window Leclerc fainted and was immediately put back to bed.

Upon further examination of the patient, the doctor this time pronounced the dread words: the General did indeed have the Siamese Fever. This time there was no hope of recovery; all around him knew the Governor General would die.

Leclerc lay miserable and in terrible pain for two days drifting in and out of delirium. Pauline never left his side during this dreadful time, taking short naps on a divan set up beside the bed, eating little from the trays that were constantly sent up to the bedchamber.

Odette hovered outside the dying man's room, only returning to the quarters she shared with her husband to wash and change her clothes.

October passed into November and the General lingered on. He regained full consciousness on November 2, and remained lucid for most of the day and into the evening. At 11:00 p.m. his life came to a close.

Pauline threw herself on the still body of her husband, weeping and wailing. It took the combined strength of the doctor and Odette, who finally ventured into the sick room, to pry her off. She was led into a nearby bedchamber and put to bed, with Odette keeping vigil at her side.

The next several days passed in gloom and tears, as arrangements were made to take the body of the dead general back to France for burial. His remains were embalmed and laid in a lead coffin, encased in an outer coffin of the richest wood the island had to offer. As a tribute to the love she bore her dead hero, Pauline cut off her long dark hair and had it wound around as a pillow for the head of the man known in life as the blonde Napoleon.

Within a week all was in readiness for the wife and child of Leclerc to set sail and return to France, accompanying the coffin. It was a dreary and a melancholy time for both Odette and Pauline, who realized they might very well never meet again. Fortunately the frenzy of selecting what would return with Pauline in household goods and her vast wardrobe took up much of the time, with little left over for conversations between the two women.

The morning of departure arrived. Odette and her husband would accompany Pauline, Dermide and their entourage down to the quay to see them off. The ship would sail on the noon tide, which left little time for goodbyes.

Dressed totally in black, with a heavy veil covering her shorn hair, Pauline led Dermide by the hand as they followed the coffin down the hill. All along the way stood groups of the townspeople, in silence as befitted the occasion. Heads bowed as the general's body passed by, and the people crossed themselves reverently. Pauline acknowledged the homage with brief nods right and left.

Soon, too soon, they arrived on the quay. The ship was prepared for departure and all of Pauline's goods had been loaded the night before.

An attachment of the household guard, led by Duval, lifted the coffin and bore it up the gangplank. It was stowed carefully away below decks for the return journey to France.

At the gangplank Pauline and Odette embraced for the last time. Both were openly weeping. Odette pulled away first, stepping back to let her former mistress cross the gangplank onto the ship. At the top Duval saluted her and himself went over the swaying boards back to the quay where he joined Odette. The Marine band struck up 'La Marseilles' and the canon in the fort commenced firing a salute.

The captain weighed anchor and slowly the ship pulled away from shore and out into the harbor. At the headland, she heeled over for a moment, then the sails caught the wind and she righted and lifted over the waves and into the open ocean beyond.

Odette and Duval stood on the quay until the ship turned around the headland and out of sight.

Hand in hand they turned back to their horses, awaiting them on the land. Duval helped Odette into her saddle and swung up onto his own mount. Together, they turned their horses' heads back toward the plantation and the far blue hills of home.

www.ingramcontent.com/pod-product-compliance
Lightning Source LLC
Chambersburg PA
CBHW051521170626
46811CB00002B/923